Peppe watched as a short, blond-haired woman with a perfectly toned body got out of the lead car and stood on the pier, staring at the boat, hands on her hips. Even from a distance, he could tell she was angry. And that anger made her interesting. He liked it when women got mad, it brought out the real animal in them.

She said something to her companion, then shook her head, her hair swaying and shining in the sunlight.

The man with her only smiled.

Peppe watched, for some reason not able to take his eyes off of her. She had something about her, a way of moving, the anger, the perfect body, her class. It all came together in a package that made him want her more than he'd wanted a woman in a long time.

SWEPT AWAY

A novel by KATHRYN WESLEY
Based on the screenplay by Guy Ritchie

POCKET BOOKS
New York   London   Toronto   Sydney   Singapore

An *Original* Publication of POCKET BOOKS

 POCKET BOOKS, a division of Simon & Schuster, Inc.
1230 Avenue of the Americas, New York, NY 10020

ISBN: 0-7434-6414-1

First Pocket Books printing October 2002

10   9   8   7   6   5   4   3   2   1

POCKET and colophon are registered trademarks of Simon & Schuster, Inc.

For information regarding special discounts for bulk purchases, please contact Simon & Schuster Special Sales at 1-800-456-6798 or busniness@simonandschuster.com

Printed in the U.S.A.

SWEPT AWAY

1

"JUICE?" THE STEWARD ASKED, HOLDING OUT A GLASS of fresh-squeezed orange juice.

Amber took the cold glass and handed him back the hot, damp towel he had given her a few minutes before. It had felt wonderful wiping off her face after the long night's flight. She let the first sip of orange juice take the memory of last night's gin away. She savored the wonderful, fresh flavor.

Around her the five others were waking as the smell of coffee filled the cabin of their private jet, warming it. She didn't drink coffee in the morning, but the other five did, and she liked the smell, even welcomed it.

There were always a lot of problems with flying overseas, but at least she had made sure the plane was stocked with the best liquors and food. Dinner after they had left New York and gotten to flight altitude had actually been passable, considering she had had it brought on board from Bossons, the newest, best restaurant in all of New York City. The plane was designed to serve catered food, and the cook and steward had somehow kept the meals warm and almost fresh.

But even with the good food and the good drinks, the flight from New York to wherever-they-were-now over Greece had seemed to take forever. She needed a shower, a good, comfortable bed, and eight hours of uninterrupted sleep.

Why planes could not be designed to be comfortable for long flights was beyond her. She and her husband Tony had spent a lot of money for this new, state-of-the-art private jet, and it was still uncomfortable. Why would anyone think that she was supposed to sleep in a chair that pretended to be a bed, and be comfortable?

The manufacturer of their new plane had promised the chairs were the most comfortable ever designed, made for sleeping on long trips. She would have a word or two with the president of that company when they got back. To her the chair felt as if it had lumps in it under the backs of her legs. On top of that, the headrest kept catching her hair, pulling it every time she moved, and the leather was of a low grade that stuck to her skin after a few hours. The man who designed those seats clearly must think that sleeping on a pile of rocks was heaven.

Amber moved her neck from side to side, trying to get at least a few of the kinks out. At one point during the night she had woken up with her head cocked sideways and drool on the pillow. She had had to ask for another pillow from the steward and go wash her face before she could even think of trying to get more sleep on that torture chair.

Around her the others were wiping off their faces, sipping coffee, and getting ready to land. The steward began picking up strewn blankets and locking cabinets, getting the cabin secured.

Across the aisle, Tony put a pillow away in a side compartment and started folding up a blanket. He was always doing that sort of thing, not leaving the small things for the servants to pick up as she thought he should. Every time she had mentioned it to him, he just shrugged and said nothing. He hadn't been born into money as she had. She had finally come to accept that because of that difference in background, she would never be able to teach him some things about the finer sides of being rich, the most important being "let someone else do it."

Tony had taken off his suit coat after dinner last night and opened his shirt collar. With his hair mussed from the long night, he looked almost sexy. Put together, yet not. That was the *perfect* look for him. Too bad she couldn't get him to dress and look like that more often. Even with the best suits and shoes, he always combed his hair flat, buttoned everything, and usually looked just a little too uptight for her tastes. Sometimes she wondered what she had ever seen in him.

Behind Tony was Michael, and beyond Michael was Todd. Both were good friends of Tony's, but neither was as rich, or as handsome, in her opinion. It seemed she and Tony were always taking the two of them, plus Michael's wife, Marina, along on these excursions. Tony called the group the drunk five, since most of the trips included a few nights of excessive drinking.

She didn't mind the group, actually. They had had their laughs and, in fact, she liked Marina, who was sitting in the back of the cabin. Marina had good taste, was from a fine Boston family, and could shop with the best of them.

Because of Marina's background, Amber often found herself pushing for that one special difference that only her money could buy. She knew it when she was doing it but so far hadn't stopped. Marina could outclass her, but Amber had the money that could buy class. And if Amber had her choice, she'd take the money any day.

Todd always seemed to be the problem person on the trips, and this time was turning out to be no exception. He was often crude, and never failed to irritate Amber by his choice of low-class dates. This trip he had brought along a very young, very stupid girl named Debi. Clearly Todd's attraction to her was below the neck, since there was nothing above Debi's neck besides a little too much makeup, blond hair, and empty blue eyes.

Amber had no idea where he met these girls, or if he was paying for them to come along, and she didn't really want to know. But so far not a one of them had lasted longer than a few weeks in Todd's life.

Halfway through last night's meal on the plane, Amber had decided that not even Todd would pay for Debi. No one would pay good money for a date who was as stupid as Debi seemed to be. At the airport, Michael, joking around, had convinced Debi that the only reason Tony had bought this new plane was because Amber wanted extra luggage space.

Amber had to admit that the extra luggage space had been a factor in buying this new jet, but not that much of one. It sure hadn't been the seats. But Debi had completely believed him about Amber's reason for buying a new jet.

Saying Debi was dumb was complimenting her.

Amber moved her head to the right, pulling on her left shoulder with her right hand, doing an exercise her trainer had shown her how to do. The exercise succeeded in releasing another kink in her neck, but nothing more. She wasn't looking forward to the flight home on these chairs. Maybe the chairs could be replaced during the two weeks they would be on the yacht. She'd talk to Tony about it later.

Amber yawned, letting her ears pop, as the pilot warned them to buckle up for landing. It was going to be good to get some fresh air and try to at least work out the knots in her back muscles from the long night. She had demanded a fully equipped gym where they were going. She was going to need it.

She took the last sip of her orange juice and handed the glass back to the steward.

Outside the light seemed extra bright, the air clear. She could see rock-covered mountains in the distance, with short olive trees and white buildings scattered up the slopes like white sand on a brown blanket. It looked like Greece. Nothing new. She'd been here at seventeen and then again five years ago. The first time was exciting, the second time boring. This time Tony had promised her something really new and exciting. They were going to be exploring islands on a cruise from Greece to Italy. She had to admit it did sound like fun, but not something she would call exciting.

The plane touched down gently and braked. Outside the window she could see shacks and maintenance hangars along the runway. A few of the shacks even had laundry hanging on clotheslines.

She turned away. There was nothing that interested her about living poorly. She knew people did, but she didn't care.

"You getting excited?" Tony asked, smiling at her as he buckled his seat belt.

"Yeah, sure," she said, ignoring her seat belt and staring at where the steward was sitting at the front near the closed cockpit door.

This trip had been Tony's idea, and he had planned it all. Touring some islands with beautiful beaches and old ruins was what she remembered him describing. Their previous vacations to different places around the world had never gone well, but as long as there were comfortable beds, she would deal with it. She had promised Tony she would try to enjoy herself this time.

The plane swung around near a fence and stopped, rocking gently. As she was about to stand, some movement outside caught her eye, and she focused on what was on the runway.

"What are those?" Amber demanded, pointing out the window at three cars sitting there on the tarmac. All three cars were pointed at the plane, clearly waiting for them to arrive.

The cars were old Mercedes sedans, all painted black. All three looked as if they had been through a war, with dents and faded paint. She hadn't been in a Mercedes that old since her high school prom.

"We are in Greece now, dear," Tony said, glancing out at what she was pointing at, then standing and retrieving his travel bag. "New cars take some time to reach here."

"Decades, from the looks of it," Amber said, disgusted.

"They do?" Debi asked, standing beside Amber in the aisle and looking out the window as if her pea-sized brain even understood what the problem was.

"That's because they have to drive them all the way from the States," Amber said. "Isn't it, Debi?"

Tony shook his head at Amber, but she ignored him.

Amber had teased Debi last night over dinner, and she figured that continuing to tease her might be the best entertainment this trip was going to offer.

"Can you drive all the way from the States?" Debi asked, looking puzzled.

Amber almost snorted through her nose. It was too easy. No sport at all.

"I'll explain it later," Todd said to Debi, patting the dumb blonde on the shoulder as he smiled at Amber.

Amber picked up her small travel purse and headed for the now open door. Between trying to sleep in chairs and having old cars pick them up, this trip was not starting off real well. But she had promised Tony she would try to enjoy herself, so try she would.

Heat washed over Amber as she emerged into the bright, clear light. It looked as if it was around midday local time, and was going to get warmer before it got cooler. The air smelled of olive trees and jet fuel.

The sun felt good on her face. She took a deep breath and let some of the tension fade away. Maybe this might be fun after all. She had forgotten how wonderful the air was in Greece, and how bright and clear the light.

She made it to the bottom of the stairs and stopped, looking around at the mountains and airplane hangars. Greece was exactly as she remembered it. Rock mountains, white buildings, clear blue skies. Beautiful, even from the runway of an airport.

"Oh, God," Marina said as she came out of the plane and saw the old cars for the first time. "Are we supposed to ride in *those?*"

"Talk to my husband," Amber said as one of the drivers in a knockoff suit indicated she should climb into the back of the lead car.

"I'll just stand out here until the luggage is loaded," Amber said, staring at the cracked leather seats of the old Mercedes. Who knew what had spilled on those seats, and she had no intention of sitting on them one moment longer than she had to.

* * *

The drive from the airport was thankfully quick, since the cars smelled of sweat, poorly masked with some sort of cleaner. The air-conditioning was loud and didn't really cool the car. Just as with the chairs in the plane, after a few minutes she found the backs of her legs sticking to the old leather of the seat.

Amber and Tony were in the lead car with their luggage, while Michael and Marina followed, and Todd and Debi brought up the rear in the last car.

The driver of Amber's car, a man who had seen his best years decades earlier, didn't seem to notice their existence. He didn't smell as bad as some New York cabbies, but he looked as if his razor had given up the fight weeks ago. He said nothing and never bothered to even look in the rearview mirror. His driving was jerky and his braking sudden. Overall, this was a highly unpleasant ride.

Tony stared at the houses flashing past and said nothing for the entire car ride. That was fine with Amber, since she didn't feel up to conversation. She had no doubt that nothing nice would come out of her mouth at this point anyway, and since she had promised Tony she would try to have fun, saying nothing was the wiser course.

The three cars wound their way through a few miles of narrow streets, bumped down a rocky slope that didn't really look like a road, and emerged out onto a long wooden pier. Their driver swung the car around, facing back toward the town, and stopped.

"This is it," Tony said, smiling at Amber as he climbed out of the car. He actually looked happy to be there.

Amber could feel the dread creeping into her stomach like a case of food poisoning. There wasn't anything close by that could be "it" as Tony had said. No big yacht, no men waiting to take their bags.

She slowly climbed out of the car, letting the warm sun and salty air calm her as she looked around. There was nothing on this dock but a few fishing boats.

"Where is our tour ship?" Amber asked. "How long are we going to have to wait?"

Tony pointed at the largest of the boats tied up to the dock near where the cars had stopped. "That's it right there."

He had to be kidding.

Amber looked at him, then back at the boat.

The thing was tiny. It had only a few deck levels and couldn't be much longer than their Hampshire pool. She remembered that Tony had said they would have a tour yacht. Well, this boat was the size of some smaller yachts at home, but far older. "Ancient" would describe it better.

The crew working on deck didn't even have uniforms. Wasn't there anything new in Greece?

Marina got out of her car and stopped.

"What's that?" she asked, glancing around at where Michael stood, smiling.

"That's where you are spending the next two weeks," Michael said. He clearly had been aware of what they were doing, but Marina hadn't. More than likely that was the only reason Marina was with them.

Amber watched the look of shock cross Marina's face as she stared at the boat.

"I did not fly all the way from New York City to wherever the fuck we are to board that," Amber said to Tony, the anger just barely held in check below the surface.

"How many vacations have we been on that you actually enjoyed?" Tony asked, working to help the driver get the luggage out of the back of the car.

She didn't answer. She hadn't liked anything they'd tried lately, and this didn't look like anything that would change that pattern.

Tony dropped a bag on the pier next to her. "Now try to keep your promise and have a good time. It was you who came up with the idea of trying something new. Remember?"

"New?" Amber said, pointing to the sailboat. "Tell me how fuckin' new is that. It's got a fuckin' chimney, Anthony."

"Well," Tony said, "it's a funnel, actually, honey. We're here now, so shall we just try to enjoy it?"

"I agreed to take part in this ridiculous idea if they had a fully equipped gym," Amber said. "I can hardly wait to see where they're hiding it."

"They have it," Tony said. "That I was assured of."

Marina headed toward the boat, leaving her bag behind, stopping right next to Amber.

"I am so sorry, Marina," Amber said, trying her best not to imagine how mad Marina was going to be by the time this was over. Marina didn't do well with roughing it, and from the looks of this, roughing it was going to be part of this vacation.

"How quaint," Marina said.

"Wonderful," Amber said to herself, soft enough that no one could hear. "Just fuckin' wonderful."

Giuseppe "Peppe" Esposito watched as the three Mercedes pulled up and stopped on the pier. He'd never had a chance to ride in anything that nice. Someday, maybe. If his luck got better. Maybe he could even get a job driving one. He knew the town pretty well, and most of the back streets and short-cuts. He'd make a good driver, but he'd miss the sea and fishing. Maybe he could do both.

He went back to sweeping, finishing up quickly to make sure the deck was clean for the passengers. He had been lucky to get this job. The captain had said over a drink that he needed an extra hand and a good fisherman to help with the six "important people" from the United States. He was going to pick them up in Greece and bring them back to Italy.

The captain had been slightly drunk and bragging that he was a big enough boss to need to hire more men. Peppe had been standing there drinking and had just happened to hear.

Peppe had spent his last money buying the captain a drink, talking to him about how good a fisherman he was, and he had gotten the job. They had left for Greece the next morning.

Since Louisa had kicked him out, he had needed a place to live and a job. Louisa had a temper like no other woman he had ever seen. When she was in a mood her green eyes flared and her voice rose and he loved her even more. Usually their arguments ended in the best sex he could have ever imagined. But lately it hadn't worked that way. She had said she had had enough of his lazy ways. Either he got a job or got out.

He got out, and then got this job. Three days' fast sail from Italy to Greece, then two weeks going from island to island, waiting on the Americans, all for good pay. The captain told him that all he had to do was follow orders, work hard, catch decent-sized fish, and stay out of the way.

Peppe could do that, then he would find a new place to live when he got back. Louisa would be sorry she had ever pushed him out the door. He would show her.

Peppe watched as a short, blond-haired woman with a perfectly toned body got out of the lead car and stood on the pier, staring at the boat, hands on her hips. Even from a distance, he could tell she was angry. And that anger made her interesting. He liked it when women got mad, it brought out the real animal in them.

She said something to her companion, then shook her head, her hair swaying and shining in the sunlight.

The man with her only smiled.

Peppe watched, for some reason not able to take his eyes off of her. She had something about her, a way of moving, the anger, the perfect body, her class. It all came together in a package that made him want her more than he'd wanted a woman in a long time.

Suddenly a hand smacked his shoulder.

"Quit staring at the boss-lady and put that broom away," the captain said in Italian, his voice cold and to the point. "Then stand by to help with luggage."

Peppe nodded and without saying anything moved to do as he was told. He had learned quickly on the trip from Italy that the best way to deal with the captain was let him do all the talking. Peppe could be the quiet type if he needed to be, and on this trip, that was exactly what he was going to be.

He stored the broom in the galley and then went back topside to watch the visitors come aboard. For some reason, all he could do was stare at the blonde with the angry eyes and wonderful, golden skin.

2

SINCE THERE WAS NO OTHER CHOICE, AMBER FOL-
lowed Tony toward the gangway leading onto the
yacht. She felt like a prisoner being lead to a death-
row cell. She swore to herself that from this day forward, she would pay attention when Tony had his
wild ideas about doing something new. Granted,
she had said she wanted new and different, but this
kind of roughing it wasn't what she had had in
mind. She was sure of that. For her, roughing it was
staying at a Hilton and having the maid service be
late.

"Welcome aboard, Professor, madam," a big, loud-
voiced Italian said in decent English. "I am your captain. You can call me . . ." He seemed to pause for a
moment, as if thinking about exactly what they could
call him, then said, "Captain."

Amber shook her head in disgust. This guy was

no rocket scientist. He and Debi should be able to have some great conversations.

The captain extended his hand to Tony and then gestured that they should go on board.

"Thank you," Tony said. "I am not actually a professor."

"That's not what I hear," the man said, smiling.

Amber had no doubt that by the time she left this stinking boat she was going to be very, very sick of that man's smile and his booming voice.

The boat looked as if it was divided into three main deck areas. At the front seemed to be a sundeck, with lounge chairs and a few small tables. The center area of the boat was empty at the moment, but was big enough to hold a decent-sized table for exterior dinners. The aft end of the boat had another deck, higher than the others, with more chairs.

"Are you a real captain, Captain?" Debi asked.

The captain frowned, not knowing exactly how to answer such a stupid question. He looked like he had just misunderstood, but Amber had to hand it to him, the guy kept smiling.

She moved up beside Tony as they boarded. "I am not interested in shaking Blackbeard's hook," she said, low enough so that only Tony could hear. "I just want to know where my cabin is."

Tony nodded and glanced around at the captain as

he followed them on board. "Captain, could you show my wife to her quarters?"

"Of course, Professor," he said.

He glanced around and then snapped his fingers, saying something in Italian to a crewmember. Then he turned to Amber. "Giuseppe here will show you to your room."

Amber nodded and then glanced up into the dark, piercing eyes of the most beautiful man she had ever seen. He looked rugged, as if he belonged on a boat. He wore white pants and a nice-fitting navy blue shirt. His skin was tanned and his face weatherworn just enough to make it handsome. His dark beard and dark, longish hair framed his face perfectly.

Her stomach clamped up, as if she had just seen her prom date in high school. Their gazes locked, and for a moment she thought he knew everything about her. Her knees felt weak and she forced herself to look away and take a deep breath.

What had just happened couldn't be. He was just a common sailor. Italian on top of that. *A common Italian sailor!* she almost screamed inside her head. He was not someone she could ever be attracted to.

She broke the look, glancing at Tony as the man picked up their luggage. Even though the moment had seemed to last a long time, it actually hadn't. Tony was still smiling at the captain, and of course, the captain was smiling back.

"This way, please," the man said, his voice deep and rough. It sent chills down Amber's spine. Suddenly the day seemed much warmer than it had a few moments ago.

He moved off, carrying some of their suitcases. Amber let Tony follow first, almost afraid to fall in behind the crewman. She couldn't remember the last time she had had a reaction like that to a man.

And this time the strong reaction wasn't helping her mood. Not only was she going to be stuck on an old boat for two long weeks, but she had no doubt that man was going to bother her the entire trip. She could see it in his eyes.

She could feel her anger boiling, but somehow she managed to hold it inside and say nothing.

He opened a low door and led them down a narrow corridor in the front area of the boat, somehow managing to not bang their luggage too badly on the walls. Then he opened a side door labeled in Italian and disappeared inside.

By the time they followed, the sailor had put their suitcases against the bulkhead and was smiling at them. His smile lit up his face even more, as if he was hiding secrets that only time with him would reveal.

Amber forced herself to look away and study the cabin. She had to admit that it was bigger than she had expected from looking at the outside of the boat. And even though it was older, the cabin had a warm charm about it, with polished wood and a large bed.

But what it didn't have was storage, at least as far as she could see. There were still four suitcases and three other smaller bags sitting beside the trunk of the Mercedes.

"Where am I going to put all my clothes?" she asked, managing to not look at the sailor as she moved to a small closet and opened it, inspecting the tiny space.

"I am sure they will find some room," Tony said as he inspected the inside of the small bathroom off the bedroom.

"Well," Amber said, pulling open a drawer, "ask Guido, or whatever his name is, to do something about it."

She glanced up at the sailor, who was watching her with those intent dark eyes that seemed to dig right into her. He smiled and kept staring at her, almost undressing her with his gaze.

The sailor then spun around and opened two cabinets behind him, showing them to her. "What you can't fit in here, you can keep in my room."

Amber stared at the man, amazed. The guy was serious, almost. She could see a twinkle of laughter in his eyes. And that made her even angrier. How dare a common man like him make fun of her?

"I am sure we can make do," she said, keeping her

voice low and controlled, as if she were speaking to a child.

"Well then," the man said, still smiling as he brushed past her and headed for the door, "if that should be all?"

She said nothing, trying not to think about the slightly musky smell of him she had caught as he passed. It was a wonderful scent that she had no doubt she could get lost in.

He stopped in the door and turned to look her in the eyes again.

"My name is Giuseppe," he said.

The name came from his firm mouth like poetry, the word flowing clear and bright. It was a name she would remember, but never let him know that she did.

He went on, smiling. "You can call me Peppe for short. I am the fisherman for the trip, but if you should need anything, I am your man."

Amber let the moment hold a little too long. Then, as the guy waited, she turned to Tony. "Ask him about the gym. I want to see the gym."

She glanced at the sailor, who she knew clearly understood the question. But there was no way she was going to ask him directly. In fact, she was going to make an extra effort to stay as far away from this Italian fisherman as she could on a small boat. It was the only safe thing to do.

"Ahh, yes, the gym," Tony said, shaking his head but playing along with the charade of him talking to the hired help. "Giuseppe, could you show my wife the gym?"

"Certainly," Peppe said. "I will go get it." He disappeared out into the narrow corridor.

"Get it?" Amber asked, turning and looking at Tony, not at all liking the sound of that. What kind of gym could he bring to her? She wasn't sure she wanted to know.

Tony only shrugged and began unpacking his clothes.

Everything about this trip was going wrong and she was barely holding it together as it was. She needed the gym to work out the tension and muscle ache. They had promised a gym, and she had better goddamned get a gym. Or someone was going to pay.

She stood there, letting the anger build, waiting.

Peppe knew right from the moment that he had first entered the kitchen that it was going to be the best place on all the boat. The small room smelled of freshly baked bread, spicy soups, and baking fish. What more could a man want in a kitchen? Especially after dealing with crazy Americans like the passengers who had just come aboard. He had no doubt he would be hiding in here, or in the crew quarters, a lot during the next two weeks.

The six American passengers had arranged for their own cook, and the captain was talking to him when Peppe entered. The guy was short and bald. But from what the captain had said, the guy was one of the best chefs in all of Italy, and was getting paid more than all of them combined for the two weeks. The crew was going to get to eat what he cooked as well, a bonus Peppe had not expected.

"What happened?" the captain asked, turning to face Peppe. "What was all the screaming about?"

Peppe laughed, moving over to sniff a freshly baked loaf of bread. He desperately wanted to pull off a hunk and stuff it in his mouth, but he refrained. "She's crazy, that woman."

"But what was the screaming about?" the captain asked.

Peppe told him how he'd gotten the two settled, offered to find extra storage space for their clothes. Then he said, "She wanted to see the gym, so I told her I would get it." Peppe moved over and sniffed a pot of tomato and garlic–smelling stew. "I thought she would have liked that, me bringing the gym to her."

"Then what?" the captain asked.

"So I brought the bicycle contraption to her and tried to show her how it worked," Peppe said, shrugging.

"And?" the cook asked, clearly as interested in the story as the captain.

"She didn't much like it," Peppe said, "so I showed her the jump rope and how it should work."

"And?" the captain asked, starting to smile.

Peppe again shrugged. "She just started screaming."

Both the captain and the cook laughed.

"She said she was going to hang you with the jumping rope," Peppe said, smiling at the captain.

The captain suddenly stopped laughing. "Me?"

Peppe nodded. "I told you she was a crazy one, that woman."

The dining table was set on the ship's deck, under the stars. They had left port hours ago, and now the only lights were over the table and on a distant island, leaving the stars bright and clear, more than Amber had ever seen before. The moon wasn't up yet, and the sky seemed to be painted almost solid with stars.

The early-evening air was still warm, and the breeze from the ship moving gently through the calm ocean was just enough to be refreshing. Overhead some birds squawked, adding another background noise to the occasional creaking of the ship's hull and the sounds of silverware being placed on the table. The waves occasionally slapped against the side of the hull, but not enough to distract.

Amber had told the group they were to dress up for each dinner, to bring some class to this wooden barge they were on. Marina wore a stunning gown that Amber had never seen before. Both the men were in open-necked jackets. Debi had on a dress that made her look more like a hooker than Todd's girlfriend. Tony had not yet finished dressing and come up on deck.

"Well, I wasn't very happy," Amber said, telling the story of the gym as they sat down. She had her second martini on the table in front of her and was slowly starting to unwind from the trip and the events getting on board. "I mean, what kind of gym could he possibly carry?"

"Yeah, good point," Todd said, snapping his napkin to open it.

"There are some modern gyms that can be carried," Michael said. He took a sip of the water placed in front of him, nodded and set the glass down. "Multitrainers, you know."

"Watching infomercials again?" Todd asked, laughing.

"So what happened next?" Marina thankfully asked before the men could get started on the joys of infomercials. Amber had been in that conversation once too often.

"He brought me some old bike thing that I am sure was ancient before I was born," Amber said. "It had grease on it and everything. Not a chance I could use it, even if I knew how."

"So you screamed?" Michael asked, smiling at her.

Amber gave him a look, then said, "Actually, I was pretty understanding. Right up until the hairy crewman pulled out a rope and told me I could jump over it."

Everyone laughed.

"A jump rope?" Michael asked, shaking his head. "I guess that makes sense on a boat this size."

"Why?" Debi asked, looking at Michael.

"You ever tried to jump rope on a boat, Debi?" Amber asked.

"No," the blank-eyed blonde said, shaking her head and clearly thinking much too hard for such a simple question. "I don't think I have."

"Do you know what jumping rope is?" Amber asked.

Debi started to giggle. "Isn't it when you . . . you know?"

Amber just stared across the table at Debi as she struggled with the question. The night around them seemed to grow darkly silent.

Silence.

"No, actually I don't," Debi finally said, staring defiantly at Amber. "But I have been skydiving before."

Amber shook her head, laughing. Too easy. Picking on this brainless wonder was just too easy.

"Where's Tony?" Todd asked, clearly trying to shift the attention away from his very stupid date.

"Yes, where is Tony?" Michael asked. "They're about to serve the first course. Not like Tony to miss a meal."

"I am sure you can live without him for just a few minutes more," Marina said, patting her husband's hand.

"You know," Debi said, still staring at Amber, "this is a great idea. Going from Greece to Italy. Have you seen the amount of deserted islands we can visit? You can't do that in the Caribbean."

"What are you going to do on a deserted island, Debi?" Marina asked, winking at Amber.

Both Todd and Michael just shook their heads and looked away.

"I'm sure I can think of something," Debi said, smiling at Marina.

"What?" Marina asked, pushing.

Amber wanted to hear the answer to this question. It was going to be good.

"What, what?" Debi asked, clearly getting confused.

Amber could not believe that a walking, talking woman could be as stupid as Debi. Besides the large chest, Amber had no idea what Todd saw in her, let alone why he would want to spend two weeks with her.

"What is it that you can think of?" Marina asked.

Debi's smile left her face as she went into thought. It looked almost painful from Amber's place at the table.

"She'd be all right," Amber said. "Wouldn't you, Debi? You'd make friends and find a nightclub, wouldn't you?"

Debi's face brightened up as she looked at Amber. "It's a deserted island, silly. Like no people. How could I go to a nightclub with no people?"

Again Todd broke into the Debi disaster. "And here he is. Nice outfit, pal. Very native."

Amber glanced over as Tony came up from below deck. He was wearing a loud, patterned Hawaiian shirt and white pants. She had never seen him look so stupid. She could feel the flush go up over her face. How could he do something like that to her?

Marina looked over at him and actually almost choked. Somehow she managed to not laugh.

"What the hell have you come as?" Amber asked. "Popeye?"

"When in Rome . . ." Tony said, smiling at everyone and moving around the table to take his seat beside Amber.

"We're in the middle of the fuckin' ocean," Amber said, shaking her head in disgust as he sat down. "What does Rome have to do with anything?"

He patted her hand as it rested on the table, then smiled at her. "I don't think there is any need for that, darling," he said. "I like this outfit. I thought it was very Errol Flynn."

"Who's Errol Flynn?" Debi asked.

"I thought we agreed that we were going to get dressed up for dinner?"

Tony only shrugged and unfolded his napkin.

Amber pushed the issue. She hated it when he made her feel stupid. "If you're going to put us on a boat built for savages, can we at least not dress like them?"

"I changed my mind," Tony said, smiling at Todd. "I wanted to be more comfortable."

"Well," Amber said, "where does that leave me? And our guests? I mean, where would we all be if we just did things because we felt like it?"

"On vacation?" Todd asked.

3

THE SMELLS FROM THE KITCHEN WERE SO RICH, PEPPE was convinced he could gain weight just being in the room. The chef, whom Peppe didn't think had a name other than "chef," wasn't allowing anyone to sample, at least not until the guests were served. Something about bad luck and bad manners. Peppe thought it a stupid rule, but he wasn't about to argue. The food smelled far too good to take a chance of not getting any.

For the last ten minutes Peppe had stood beside the captain at the door leading from the kitchen out onto the deck where the six Americans were seated. They had been listening to the conversation, especially the woman's point of view on the story of the gym.

The captain shook his head in disgust as the woman who screamed at Peppe said, "Was I speaking to you, Todd?"

Peppe could feel the coldness in her voice all the way into the warm kitchen.

The captain let the door close so that the voices from the table were muffled. "She's a piece of work," the captain said, clearly feeling as disgusted as Peppe felt.

The chef laughed. "Not much of a vacation coming up for poor old Tony."

"Never mind Tony," Peppe said. "What about me? It's all right for you in here. Vegetables don't talk back. But I have to go out there and wait on *that* woman."

He had drawn the unlucky spot to be the waiter the first night. And after what had happened with the gym, none of the other crewmembers would trade with him for a different night.

Peppe indicated the outfit the woman had wanted him to dress up in to serve dinner, then stared at the captain, who was barely managing to contain a smile. "Please, Captain, would you look after that one?"

The captain actually laughed. "Just remember who's paying you and what you're getting paid to do."

Peppe shook his head. "I was doing just fine without the money. I was happy, thank you."

"Of course you were, Peppe," the captain said, laughing. "Now pick up that tray and try not to drop anything on that woman."

"Would it matter?" Peppe said, shrugging. "She's going to yell at me no matter what I do."

The captain gave him a look, so Peppe did what he was told, putting on his best smile as he went through the door and into the night air. In all his life he had never felt so foolish. He was a fisherman, not a waiter. It was going to be a long evening.

Amber sat on the bench on one end of what the captain had called a dinghy. To her it was just a big rubber raft with wooden seats. Nothing more. It was yellow, with black stripes and plastic anchors where ores could be put on. The oars were at the moment in the bottom of the dinghy, banging her ankles every time she moved wrong.

The seats in the raft were weathered. There was no telling how many splinters she was going to have to take out of her skin later. If she had her guess, the dinghies were left over from the Second World War. More than likely the captain had bought them surplus.

The hairy Italian sailor who had offered her the jump rope and then had the gall to wait on them last night at dinner was sitting at the other end near the outboard motor. Another deckhand was beside him, and two other crewmen were in the other dinghy.

The man had blissfully been silent so far. Amber found herself glancing at him, just as she had done while he served dinner. And the more often she caught herself looking at him, the angrier she got. Both at him and herself.

Tony had suggested a swim and everyone had been excited about it, so the captain had anchored just off an island that looked more like a big rock than a landmass. Against her better judgment, they had all climbed into the two rubber rafts and found this deserted cove.

Amber had to admit the cove was beautiful, surrounded by high rocks and a few palm trees, but there was no way she was getting in that water. There was no telling what was in there, or what creatures lived down there. It was so clear that the sand and rocks below the raft looked very, very close, even though one of the crewmen had told Tony it was still twenty meters deep.

"What's wrong with Amber?" Debi asked as she treaded water beside Michael, Todd, and Tony. Marina had just made a surface dive and Amber could tell she was about ten feet under, studying something on the bottom with her mask.

Debi looked exactly like Amber had imagined she would in a bathing suit. The girl might not have taste in clothes or men, or a brain the size of an ant's, but she knew how to pick a suit that made the best of her full assets. There wasn't a fraction of an inch of cloth in that suit that wasn't filled out perfectly. Amber felt almost plain beside her. And old.

And feeling old didn't help her mood, either.

Amber ignored Debi's question, pretending she couldn't hear, even though the only noise in the cove was the gentle lapping of the waves on the rocks. There weren't even birds around this place. And sound traveled over the smooth water like music in a fine concert hall.

"Yeah," Todd asked as Marina surfaced with a gasp. "Are you sure your wife's all right?"

"What's wrong, darling?" Tony shouted, even though just speaking in a normal voice would have been clear enough.

"Come on in," Michael shouted as well, waving at her. "It's gorgeous."

"I'm not getting in with all that shit in there," Amber said, her voice colder than she had intended it to sound. Just being in the same raft with the hairy Italian fisherman was putting her on edge.

Tony looked around, pretending to search for something floating beside him. Finally he shouted, "What shit?"

Michael laughed and Amber turned away, ignoring them. She took out her sun umbrella and flipped it open. She had had enough sun for the moment. No point in damaging her skin, especially this early in the trip.

"It's not going to rain, madam," Peppe said.

She looked at him, puzzled.

He raised his eyes and looked at her umbrella, then smiled at her.

She loved his smile, his entire look, yet she couldn't let herself even think about him. She was still angry about the gym, and the idea that she, of all people, could even be attracted to some lowlife like this Italian fisherman.

"Is that a joke?" she asked, staring at him.

He just smiled and said nothing. For an instant she thought he was toying with her. Then she realized who she was dealing with and knew that couldn't be possible. He was just a fisherman. He wouldn't dare toy with her.

"Come on in," Tony said, swimming over closer to the raft. "It's clean as a whistle."

"Depends on who's been blowing the whistle, doesn't it?" Amber said.

Tony just shook his head and swam back toward Michael and Todd and Debi.

"Don't bother, sweetie," Marina said to Amber, waving Tony away as she treaded water off to one side of the raft. "It's really wet."

Amber knew that was just Marina being nice to her.

The Italian sailor offered Amber a mask and snorkel like the ones Marina and the others were using. "Put a mask on and swim with the fishes," he said, again smiling at her. "You'll enjoy swimming with the fishes."

"Why?" Amber asked, staring at him with her best cold stare.

He didn't even seem to notice. He just kept smiling at her. "'Cos it's nice swimming with the fishes."

"Well," Amber said, pushing the mask away, "when you have some time off I suggest you swim with the fishes."

She turned away, facing her husband and friends in the water. "And *fish* is the plural for fish."

The hairy Italian's laugh echoed over the water and mixed with the talking and laughter coming from her husband in the water.

She liked the Italian's laugh better, but not in a thousand years would anyone ever know that.

And she hated the fact that he was laughing at her.

4

AMBER'S LONG MORNING OF SITTING IN A RUBBER RAFT
had finally ended, without her getting one splinter in
her ass off the rough wooden seats. She was amazed
by the luck.

The hours stuck in that uncomfortable position
had given her muscle cramps, and by the time she
got back to the boat she had decided that it didn't
matter how old that exercise bike was, she desperately needed to use it. It was going to be the only
way she was going to stay sane on this trip. So she
had ordered the antique cycling machine cleaned up,
the oil and grease removed, and the seat polished.
Then she had had the old thing brought up on deck
and put beside the front lounge chairs, facing out
over the waves.

She had changed into her exercise shorts and put
on a bikini top. There, with the wind from the ship's

movement keeping her cool, she worked out the soreness in her legs and back while she stared out over the beautiful ocean.

Todd and Debi had joined her, just about the time she had finally gotten started. They had settled in on chaise longues and begun reading the paper. Behind her, along the rail, the hairy Italian fisherman was cleaning the railing. She had no idea what he was using, other than it smelled awful, like an open sewage line in New York on a hot day.

But for the moment it wasn't the fisherman, or even her pedaling on the old exercise bike, or even the wind whipping her hair that had her attention. It was something Todd had said while reading the paper.

He had started with a simple statement about how the rich just got richer and the entire world wanted to move to the United States and get rich.

"And what's wrong with that?" Amber had asked, pulling her pace back slightly so she could talk and pedal at the same time. "It's the nature of capitalism."

"But there are problems raised by capitalism," Todd had said. "Don't you agree?"

Amber had laughed. "What problems?"

And that got the discussion off and running.

"Your old man is the boss of an enormous pharmaceutical company," Todd said. "His company has to make a profit to keep the shareholders happy."

"So?" Amber said, not really catching his point as to why that was a bad thing.

"That's not necessarily in the public's interest," Todd said, sitting up and staring at her as if that would help her get his meaning.

"If the public's interested," Amber said, "they can buy the stock. What's your point?"

Todd shook his head and gave his paper to Debi to hold so that it wouldn't blow off the boat. Then he turned and faced Amber, sitting sideways on the chair. "Let's imagine that there is a drug that can remedy a certain kind of blindness. Now, even though the drug costs the company almost nothing to manufacture, they set a high price in the name of capitalism."

"So?" Amber asked again.

"Unless you can afford the drug, you're going to stay blind," Todd said. "That's not in the public's best interest."

"They would have stayed blind without the company coming up with, and manufacturing, the drug anyway," Amber said. "What's to stop them from getting a job and buying the drug like everyone else?"

"They're blind," Todd said.

"So what?"

"Well," Todd said, shaking his head at her, "don't you think that limits their employment opportunities a little?"

"They could bake cakes," Amber said, remembering a chef she had once read about who was almost blind and did the best cakes and pies in all of New York.

"They can't all bake cakes," Todd said.

"I'm still not following your point," Amber said. "You wouldn't ask a tire company to fit out everybody's cars in the country for free, would you?"

Todd just shook his head. "You have to agree that it does raise some ethical questions."

"Ethical?" Amber said, disgusted, pushing her pace back up to almost a sprint. "The laws of capitalism are that the proprieter of goods can set any price he or she sees fit, and shall not be at the mercy of any moral issues. You can't afford the drugs to help yourself, well, get out there and bake some cakes so that you can."

"Whose quote is that?" Todd asked.

"Mine."

She turned away from Todd and just stared out over the water, pedaling as fast as she could. She hated discussions like that, and never really saw the point in them.

Todd snorted, lay back, and covered his eyes.

Beside him Debi just looked confused.

The captain had come up beside Peppe as the argument wound up. Peppe had heard every word of it, and he had no doubt that almost everyone on the boat had heard that woman's last pronouncement, she had shouted it so loudly.

"I can't see her baking too many cakes," Peppe said, softly enough that only the captain could hear.

The captain laughed and said nothing.

"She is without heartbeat, that woman," Peppe said, disgusted. "She's a lizard."

He hated the fact that he was attracted to her. He hated the fact that all the woman he was attracted to had mean streaks in them. But at the same time, he loved it. Women who could stand up to him excited him.

"Stop moaning, Peppe," the captain said. "You are not married to her."

"A lizard, I tell you," Peppe said. "One that should be made into a bag, belt, and boots."

At that moment she turned and looked right at him, then snapped her fingers. "You!" she shouted. "Guido!"

Peppe ignored her. It was bad enough that he had to wait on something so low, but he would never answer to the wrong name. He had more pride than that.

The captain smiled at him, patted him on the shoulder, and went in the opposite direction, leaving him with his cleaning and the woman snapping her fingers at him. Peppe wanted to call after the captain that he was a coward, but he didn't.

"You!" she shouted again, twisting around on the exercise bike while still pedaling.

Peppe pretended he was intent on the matters of his cleaning, ignoring her.

Beside her, out of the corner of his eye Peppe could see Todd shake his head and sit up. "Peppe?"

Peppe turned and smiled at Todd, and moving the ten steps toward where the man lay beside his very well-endowed girlfriend. He ignored the woman on the bike, acting as if she wasn't there at all.

"Yes, sir," Peppe said, stopping in front of Todd. "What can I do for you?"

"Sir is madam," Amber said before Todd could speak.

Todd shrugged and nodded in Amber's direction, indicating Peppe should take care of her.

"Yes, madam," Peppe said, turning to her and smiling.

"Water and a towel," she demanded.

"Yes, madam," he said again, still smiling at her. The fire in her eyes told him that he had won that little battle. But he had no doubt that she was a long way from being finished with him.

"And, Pee Pee," Amber said, almost sneering at him, "I want it cold, you understand? Not cool. Cold."

Under his breath, in Italian, he said as he turned away, "As cold as the blood in your veins, madam."

Marina brushed past him as he started for the galley. Behind him he heard her say, "Got some spunk in him, that seaman, hasn't he?"

Peppe smiled as Amber said, "We are going to have to watch him."

Peppe liked the game. He was watching her, she was watching him. The trip had only began. It was going to be an interesting two weeks, of that he was sure. Two weeks of hell.

Somehow, Peppe had made it through another night helping serve the six dinner and listening to the constant demands of the woman. As soon as he was allowed, he had retreated into the kitchen for a taste of the fish he had caught, baked in a way that made them seem like they had swum in heaven's waters.

He let a forkful melt in his mouth. Never had he tasted something so wonderful and light. And the white sauce over the top brought out the flavor of the catch instead of hiding it.

"Perfect," he had told the chef. "Never has my fishes tasted like that."

Of course, the chef would not give him his method of preparing the catch, but asked if possible if Peppe could deliver more of the same fish tomorrow.

"With fishing," Peppe had said, "there is never a guarantee."

"As with cooking," the chef had said, laughing.

The next morning Peppe came up to the hatch that led out to the deck. Two of the sailors whose jobs it was to watch the ship at night were standing in the doorway with the door just barely ajar, peering out.

"I'm bored," Peppe heard Amber say from the deck beyond.

"I know it," Marina said. "But we are a little fucked, aren't we? We are in the middle of the sea, with nothing but sun for distraction. Come on, lie down, have a martini, take up smoking, and swallow a couple of pills."

As Peppe watched over the heads of the other two crewmen, Amber moved to loosen her bikini strap.

He yanked the other men back and pushed the door closed silently.

"Have you no dignity?" he asked them, pretending to be harsh.

Both laughed and moved past him to go below. He knew he hadn't fooled them.

After he made sure they were gone, he eased the door open and took a longer look himself. The woman had a fine body, that much was for sure. It was just too bad such a foul personality went with it.

* * *

The quick stop at a very small fishing village on the rocky edge of a small island had at least gotten Amber some relief from the boredom. She hadn't gotten off the boat since the captain assured her there was nothing to see, but they did pick up the morning *New York Times* and supplies for the night's dinner that had been waiting for them on the small island.

From what she understood, Tony had arranged for the *Times,* good wine, and other supplies to be delivered at different locations during the entire trip. At least he had done that much right, more than likely for himself. Tony hated not starting the morning by spending time over the paper with a good cup of coffee.

Now all six of them sat silently reading at the table on the center deck, passing sections around to each other as they finished. Even Debi was engrossed in the news. Amber figured it was the boredom. Maybe even terminally stupid people could get bored enough to try to learn something.

Amber was just starting into the front page when the hairy Italian stepped on board and placed a coffeepot on the table. It was the same pot they had left mostly full at breakfast.

"What's that?" Amber asked.

"What?" the hairy Italian asked, staring at her with his piercing eyes.

"That!" Amber said, making her voice as cold and

biting as she could. She wasn't going to let him get to her this time.

He smiled at her. "It's a jug."

"No, it's a coffeepot, actually," she said. "What's in the coffeepot, Pee Pee?"

He was trapped. He couldn't ignore her getting his name wrong now, so he had to answer her. And she could tell in his eyes that he knew that she had him trapped.

"Coffee, madam."

"Reheated coffee?" Amber asked, knowing full well it was without even tasting it.

"Yes," he said.

"What am I supposed to do with that?" she demanded.

"Err, drink it?" he said.

She could see the smile trying to creep over his face, and it made her mad. He was laughing at her again. How dare he do that?

"Amber, it's not his fault," Todd said, glancing up from his section of the paper.

The hairy Italian turned and moved back toward the door of the galley, leaving the pot of coffee on the table in front of her.

"Well," Amber said, "whose fault is it, then, Todd? Who's paying whom to do what around here?"

She glanced up at the departing back of the Italian fisherman.

Tony coughed, shaking his head at her. Then he said, "Mr. Esposito."

Amber was stunned Tony remembered the man's name and treated him with respect. She hated it when her husband did that with common people. It made her feel common, too.

"Yes, sir," the Italian said, turning back and nodding respectfully to Tony.

"Could you accommodate my wife, please?"

Amber watched as the fisherman smiled. "Accommodate? Does this mean live in my house, sir? Is that what you mean?"

Amber felt the blood rise in her face. She desperately wanted to just stand and smash the stupid smile from the fisherman's face, but she said nothing.

"Oh," Marina said, raising her hand to shade her eyes from the sun and smiling at Amber. "I think that was a joke, sweetie."

"He's being rude, Anthony," Amber said.

Tony nodded, clearly not upset. In fact, Tony was doing his best to not laugh, and that just made Amber even angrier.

"Just let me deal with this, darling," Tony said after a moment.

She hated it when he said that. It was so condescending, but she kept silent.

"Would you please make my wife a fresh cup of coffee, Mr. Esposito?"

The Italian fisherman smiled and nodded. "Certainly, Professor."

With that he picked up the coffeepot, turned, and walked away.

From behind a section of the *New York Times,* Todd snorted, but managed not to laugh.

Amber just sat there, fuming. She would get even with that hairy Italian if it took her the entire trip.

5

EVEN IN THE MIDDLE OF THE DAY THE GALLEY SMELLED of rich foods and freshly baked bread. The chef was nowhere to be seen, but the captain was standing at what served as a liquor cabinet for the ship, making himself a strange green cocktail.

Peppe slammed the coffee jug down on the table and dug into the coffee supplies, getting the filter and grounds he needed to brew a fresh pot.

The captain glanced at him. "Now what is the matter with that woman? What does she want?"

Peppe held up the still almost full pot, trying his best to contain his anger and not throw the entire thing against the wall. "Perfectly good coffee isn't good enough for her. I tell you, that's enough of that fuckin' woman."

"And what would you do about her?" the captain asked, staring at Peppe, half smiling while he finished stirring his drink.

"I think I might . . ." Peppe stopped and managed to take a deep breath. Why he was letting that woman get to him was beyond his understanding. At one moment he was attracted to her, at the next all he wanted to do was strangle the life out of her. He had had lovers like that in the past, but none that felt this intense.

He shook his head and went back to putting the coffee in the filter and setting the coffeemaker to make another pot.

"You think you might what?" the captain asked, clearly trying not to laugh.

Peppe glanced at the captain, then picked up a knife from the sink. "I think I'm going to kill that fuckin' bitch with a kitchen knife. A dirty kitchen knife."

The captain actually laughed. "Giuseppe, you surprise me. Wasn't it you who told me in the bar the night I hired you that a real man's first duty was to preserve his dignity?"

"Exactly," Peppe said. "That's why I'm going to kill her with a kitchen knife. She doesn't deserve a good knife. Nothing like a fisherman's knife. She's not good enough for that."

"When you are not serving them," the captain said, "stay away from her. That way she won't be such a problem."

"That's easy for you to say," Peppe said. "She isn't

hunting you down. Everywhere I turn, there she is, even when I'm fishing. I feel like a lame gazelle stalked by the eyes of a hungry leopard, or the wilting leaf trapped in the jaws of a ravenous tortoise."

"Very theatrical," the captain said. "Now clean the boiler."

Behind him the coffee started dripping into the new pot, filling the galley with the wonderful smell of fresh beans.

Amber felt the bourbon, for some reason more than she normally did back in the city. It made her head light, but it didn't do much for her boredom. Even the poker game that Todd had suggested was getting dull.

They had set up the game in the main cabin, since the night air on deck had a bite to it. Smoke from Marina's cigarettes floated near the ceiling, forming a cloud against what looked like a polished wooden sky.

"Four thousand," Amber said, glancing at her last card to see the six that made her straight.

"Hold on," Michael said. "What just happened? We were playing for twenty dollars and now it's four thousand?"

Amber smiled at him, pretending to be a sweet thing. Only Michael and Debi were still in the hand. Todd and Tony were having a conversation as to the advantages of chemicals that she had been doing her best to ignore.

"What's the problem, Michael?" Amber asked. "Don't you think I'm good for it?"

"Tony," Michael said, glancing at Amber's husband beside him, "can't you control your wife?"

Tony shrugged and went back to the argument with Todd.

"Can't you control yours?" Amber asked, smiling at Marina as she took two pills and knocked them back with another scotch.

"Well, that much money changes the atmosphere," Michael said. "This was a fun game, remember?"

"Come on, Michael," Amber said, pushing him. "You're supposed to be Mr. Moneybags."

"I'm supposed to be on vacation," Michael said.

"Stop being such a pussy," Marina said, jabbing at her husband's arm.

"C'mon, c'mon. If you haven't got money, I'll take jewelry and shoes," Amber said.

Michael tossed his cards upside down into the pile and stood. "That's enough. I fold. I have no interest in playing 'get fucked quick' with Imelda Marcos."

"Oh, come on, Todd," Tony said, "the advantages of chemicals are obvious."

Amber shook her head as Michael left. Not even a good fight to keep her entertained. "Do we have to listen to this again?" she said to Tony.

"I'll see you," Debi said, smiling. "And your four thousand."

Amber was surprised. Debi had played very few hands over the last few hours, and had said even less.

"Big spender," Amber said. She flipped over her cards. "Straight. What have you got?"

"Full," Debi said. "Queens over."

Amber slammed her cards into the pile. Debi was the most frustrating woman on this boat. Amber glanced over at the hallway leading to the galley just as the hairy Italian fisherman came past.

"Guido?"

She watched as he stopped cold and raised his eyes at the ceiling. He was carrying a number of fish and she had no doubt he wanted to just dump them in her lap. But she also knew he didn't dare.

"Yes, madam?" he said.

"Once you put those reptiles down," Amber said, glancing at the table in front of them as she gathered up the cards and started to shuffle, "would you please empty the ashtrays?"

"Yes, madam," he said, moving on and into the galley.

By the time she had dealt the next hand to the five of them, the fisherman was back with a small dish. He started beside Marina emptying the ashtrays. Amber watched him without actually letting anyone see she was watching.

"Where would we be without fertilizer and pesticides?" Tony asked Todd as he glanced at his cards and tossed them away.

"You could ask Peppe," Todd said. "He was a full-time fisherman in a small town in Italy until pollution put an end to that area." He tossed his cards away as well.

"Oh, God," Marina said, her voice slurring, "is this a sad story?" She didn't look at her hand, but instead just called the first bet of five dollars.

"Ask him what he thinks of chemicals," Todd said.

Amber sighed. She hadn't thought this trip could get duller, and yet it had. With Todd focusing on Peppe, she was sorry she asked the Italian to do the chore he was doing.

Amber watched as Peppe shrugged.

"Peppe," Tony said, "what do you think about it? What do you think about pesticides and fertilizer?"

"Whatever," Peppe said, shrugging and moving to empty the next ashtray.

"He's busy," Amber said. "Let him get on with his job and get back to his reptiles." She glanced at the cards in her hand and raised. Nothing but garbage cards.

"Come on, Peppe," Todd said, "you must have an opinion."

Peppe glanced at Tony, then at Todd without looking at Amber. She tossed her hand away and Debi giggled as she pulled in the antes.

Peppe dumped a third ashtray into the bowl and then said, "If it's man-made, I don't trust it."

"Why?" Tony asked.

"You can't cut corners with nature," Peppe said. "Chemicals have made life easier for a few people, but easier doesn't mean better. Money corrupts people's principles. You can't see clearly when money is involved."

"Oh, no!" Marina wailed, pretending to be distraught. "Not money and principles."

"No," Tony said, "this is interesting. Go on."

Amber was appalled that her husband was giving their waiter so much attention.

Amber started to try to stop the conversation, but Tony put his hand up for her to be quiet. She sat back, fuming.

"Chemicals have made a few people very rich," Peppe said. "But as the old expression goes, there is no such thing as a free lunch. You pay now or you pay later."

"True," Todd said. "So true."

Peppe went on, much to Amber's disgust.

"The trouble is, with chemicals when you pay later you don't know how much interest you gonna be charged, and who is gonna pay it."

Todd laughed. "Very good, Peppe."

"Oh, yes," Marina said, clapping, "very good, Peppe."

"Thank you, nature boy," Amber said, disgusted that her husband and Todd had let the servant talk so long. "Now could you please finish emptying the ashtrays?"

Peppe nodded and went back to work.

Tony patted Peppe's arm. "We'll talk later."

"Grand idea," Todd said.

Amber was so horrified, she didn't know what to say.

6

PEPPE WIPED THE SWEAT FROM HIS BROW AND STOOD silently near the rail as Danny served lunch. The day had started hot and had just gotten warmer with every hour, especially with no wind from the ship's movement. The captain had the dropped sails so that the guests could sit under parasols to shade them from the sun while they ate. Peppe was just happy he wasn't the one doing the serving today. The blond woman had not let up her complaints since breakfast.

And now over lunch she was still at it.

"If the sun wasn't so hot," she said, "I just might go swimming."

"No, you wouldn't, darling," Marina said. "The water's too cold."

Peppe imagined himself tossing her into the water and smiling at her as she screamed at him. Since this morning he had been having more and more of those types of wonderful daydreams.

"I can't eat this," she said, shoving her plate aside in disgust.

"What's wrong with it?" Michael asked, chewing on the pasta.

Peppe knew it had been prepared especially at her request by the chef. It was some sort of special dish that only she and the chef knew how to make. And Peppe doubted she actually knew, even though she claimed she did.

Amber glanced around until she spotted Peppe. Even though there were three other crewmen closer, and Danny was serving them, she called for him. "Nature boy! Pee Pee."

"I think that's you," a crewman beside him said with his back turned to her. Peppe could tell he was laughing silently.

Peppe wished he could just walk away. But on a ship this size, there wasn't far to walk away to. And she had been clear that she wanted him. The captain would not be pleased if he just ignored her. And ignoring that woman always made things worse, of that Peppe had no doubt.

He pushed himself off the rail and ambled over to the table. It took him a moment and he didn't look at her, instead smiling at Danny, who was looking terrified. When he finally got close to her he said, "Yes, madam?"

"The fish is bad. It is off."

"Yes, madam," Peppe said, imagining what he really wanted to do right at that point.

"Why are you serving bad fish?" she demanded.

Now he let his mind run free as he stared at her, letting her stupid question hang in the air.

He imagined what he would do if this was a perfect world where he was in control. He would reach out, pick up the large bowl of pasta and fish, and pour it over her head.

Then he would say, "In that case, if you don't want to eat it, you probably want to wear it."

He knew she would stand and scream and stagger around, playing up her hurt to a major scene as she dug pasta and fish out of her hair and eyes.

He would love the scene. He would laugh, applaud her foolishness and her performance.

And if she screamed, "He has blinded me!" he would reply, "So now you can bake cakes."

And then Peppe knew in his imagination that she would beg to her husband, as she always did when something didn't go her way. The poor husband would stand up and start to speak.

Peppe would not let him. Peppe knew exactly what he would say to the husband in a perfect world. "Sit the fuck down, rich boy, or you'll need all the drugs you got to ease the pain I have for you."

Peppe knew the rich bitch would then scream for

her husband to do something, but Peppe, in his own perfect world, would tell her to shut up and tell it to the fishes as he picked her up and tossed her into the open sea.

"Are you listening, nature boy?" Amber asked, snapping Peppe out of his perfect daydream.

"Yes, madam," he said, even though he had not heard her last sentence, and didn't care to.

"I asked you why you served bad fish?"

Peppe decided that the question was too stupid to even respond to, so he picked up the fish and turned for the kitchen with it in his hands. He so wanted to fulfill his fantasy, but again, this boat was too small to run very far.

Peppe winked at Danny, who hadn't had the courage to move yet.

"He's not the cook, Amber," Peppe heard Tony say behind him. "He wasn't even waiting on us. Danny was."

"I'm not going to let Guido get off that easily," Amber said, her voice carrying clearly to Peppe.

"It's not a question of letting him off, darling," her husband said. "You know he's not the cook. He's not responsible."

"Not responsible, my ass," Amber said, her shout carrying out over the water. "He's had it in for us since we have been on this fuckin' raft."

At that point Peppe went through the galley door

and let it close behind him, cutting off the woman's complaining and threats. In all his life he had never hated someone as much as he now hated that woman. She was going to drive his actions far beyond daydreams if she wasn't careful.

In the galley was the chef and the captain. Both looked surprised when he came in carrying the bowl of fish.

"She's fuckin' mad," Peppe said, sliding the fish onto the center table. "She needs a doctor. A check-up from the neck up."

"Shut up, Peppe," the chef said, "and take this up."

He handed Peppe a bowl of vegetables.

"Don't tell me to shut up, you short stuff," Peppe said, staring at the surprised look on the chef's face. "You're the chef, you overcooked the fish, you could do with the exercise. You fuckin' take it up to that bitch."

The captain, who had been standing off to one side opening a bottle of wine, stepped up beside Peppe.

"What did you say?" the chef asked, stepping toward Peppe, his bulk barely fitting past the center table in the galley.

Peppe wasn't afraid of the chef, or the captain. At this point he'd be happy to be let off at the next stop and be done with the rich Americans and that woman.

"I said you take it up, midget."

Peppe stared at the chef, expecting a fight, but the chef wasn't reacting as Peppe had expected him to react.

"No, the other bit," the chef said, waving his hand in the air. "The bad bit."

"She said the fishes was bad," Peppe said, pointing at the bowl of fish.

"Bad?" the captain asked, surprised. He grabbed a piece of fish and put it in his mouth a half second before the chef did. After a moment the captain said, "It tastes okay to me."

The chef nodded.

"Of course it's okay," Peppe said. "You know she's crazy."

"Never mind," the captain said. He turned to the chef. "Make some more."

"Why?" both Peppe and the chef said at the same time.

"Because they're rich," the captain said. "All rich people play funny little games. I see it every time, every trip. Don't react, and they get bored and change the game."

"Don't react?" Peppe asked. "How?"

The captain put a blank smile on his face. "Our job is to smile like idiots."

The chef snorted and turned to put on more fish. Peppe just stared at the captain. "Tell me, Captain, how can you smile when your tongue is so far up their asses?"

"Watch and I'll show you," the captain said, smiling at Peppe's insult.

The captain took the bottle of wine, placed it in an ice bucket, and took it out the door toward the table. Peppe followed him, keeping the door slightly open so he could see and hear what was happening.

"The chef is very sorry the fish was overcooked," Peppe heard the captain say as he placed the wine at the table.

"Like hell I am," the chef said softly beside Peppe in the galley door.

The captain went on. "He'll make some new straightaway."

"Are we being punished because we are rich?" Amber asked, staring at the captain. "Is that the problem?"

Peppe could see the captain's face as he kept the stupid smile firmly in place. "No, no, I love money," he said. "If you weren't rich, we wouldn't be here in this beautiful spot in the middle of the sea."

Peppe could not believe the captain had said all that with a smile on his face.

"In fact, madam," the captain said, smiling even more, "we love you, and we love your money more."

At that everyone at the table laughed and somehow

the captain just kept smiling. Peppe was impressed and disgusted at the same time.

The blond bitch just sat there fuming, her arms crossed.

Peppe knew there wasn't a chance in hell he was going back on deck tonight.

The next day the captain's smile seemed to get even more sickly and disgusting, at least as far as Peppe was concerned.

The day was as hot as the day before, and they had put into a bay on an island that was a favorite stop for the big tour boats that cruised this area. The entire village in this bay was set up to sell to the tourists who poured off the big boats and thought they were getting a real fishing village experience. Peppe doubted that a real fishing boat had been based out of this bay in a decade. A few old ones were docked there, but only for show.

The six Americans had gone into the village earlier, and for the first time since they had boarded, Peppe felt calm. Just knowing that he wasn't going to be called some stupid name while he fished, or even see that blond-headed woman riding her bike that didn't move, was a relief.

He stood off to one side, hidden by the galley door, as they returned. He could feel his anger coming back again. He had caught four beautiful fish for the night's dinner and had just delivered them to the chef. It had been a wonderful morning without Americans. Too bad it couldn't last.

"Ahh, Professor," the captain said, the sickly smile stuck on his face. "Welcome back." He reached down toward the dinghy and helped the man on board.

"I'm not really a professor, Captain."

"Of course you are," Peppe heard the captain say, smiling.

"Ah, Captain," Marina said, letting the captain help her on board as well, "how good to see you."

Peppe watched as she handed the captain two bags of clothes and trinkets. From the looks of the packages in the dinghy, the merchants of this island had done just fine that morning.

"The pleasure is ours," the captain said, turning to hand the bags to a crewman standing close by. "Did you have a good time?"

"Fantastic," Michael said as he too was helped on board. "Thank you, Captain."

Todd was next up, struggling under the weight of more bags than any one man should carry. "You know," Todd said, "you really have some interesting ruins on these islands."

Peppe tried not to laugh. There were ruins on most of these islands, and all through Greece and Italy. The remains of an old castle and village on this island were nothing in comparison to most, but the island merchants had used the ruins to attract the ships so that they could sell the trinkets. And for Americans who never see anything older than a few hundred years, any ruin would do, it seemed.

The captain indicated that another crewman should help Todd with some of the bags he was carrying. To Peppe poor Todd seemed loaded down like a pack mule.

"Let me help you there, young lady," the captain said, ignoring Todd and turning to help Debi up out of the dinghy. Peppe shook his head as the captain managed to use both hands in his assistance.

"Are the ruins old?" Debi asked as she managed to get on board even with the captain's groping help.

"No, Debi," Marina said, disgusted, "they just built the ruins."

"They did a good job," Debi said as Peppe tried not to laugh. "Don't the ruins look old, Todd?"

Todd just shook his head and indicated that the crewman with some of his packages should follow him.

"Ahh, signora," the captain said, reaching down to help Amber out of the dinghy last, "did you have a good time?"

"Yes, I did," Amber said, ignoring his outstretched hand and getting on board herself. "Thank you, Captain."

She stopped and thrust a bag at the captain. "I found a fishmonger and bought some fresh fish. Could you give this to the chef and tell him to prepare it for tonight?"

Peppe could feel his anger boiling again. How dare she do that? She knew he caught the fish for this boat. He wanted to step toward her and shout in her face, but then he remembered what the captain had said. He should ignore the rich people's games and they will stop. But with this kind of insult, he was finding it hard to just ignore and keep smiling. He really was going to kill her some day.

The captain looked in the bag and, even though he still had the smile plastered on his face, Peppe could tell the captain didn't like what he saw.

"Madam," the captain said, "Peppe always catches the fishes for us to eat."

Amber shook her head, disgusted. "Fish is the plural for fish. I am not interested in Peppe's fish."

"I promise you," the captain said, "that Peppe's fishes are always the freshest and tastiest."

"I am not interested in his fish," she said, her voice getting to the anger stage that Peppe was coming to loathe. "Capisce?"

The captain looked at her, still smiling. "You speak Italian, madam?"

Peppe just could not take any more, either of the

captain's sickly smile or the woman insulting his fishing. If there was anything in the world that he knew, it was fishing.

"That's enough," Peppe said in Italian to the captain, striding toward the two. The rest of the Americans had gone below with their gifts.

The captain turned to Peppe and in Italian replied, "That's enough what?"

In Italian, Peppe said, "Why is this fuckin' bitch moaning about my fishes?"

"What did he say?" Amber demanded, sneering at first Peppe and then the captain. "I know that word *fuckin'*."

The captain, the smile still stuck to his face like tomato sauce after a full meal, said to the woman, " 'Fuckin' is the Italian name of the fishes, madam." The captain held up the bag she had given him. "He does not think it's a very good fishes."

"Fuckin is the name of the fish?" she asked, clearly not believing the captain.

Peppe was somehow managing to keep a straight face, but his desire to laugh at this woman was eating at the anger, draining it away.

"Yes, madam," the captain said, his face perfectly serious.

Peppe needed to remind himself to never play poker with the captain. The man could bold-face lie without even blinking a eye.

"I don't care what Peppe thinks about this *fuckin*," she said, pointing at the bag.

"But, madam," the captain said, "Peppe is looking out for your interests."

"And just how is that?" she demanded.

Peppe said nothing, hardly allowing himself to breathe for fear of breaking into laughter at the stupidity of this bitchy American.

"He is sensitive to the fact that this fishes," the captain held up the bag, "may not be as good as his fishes, and he wouldn't want to see you unhappy."

Dead, yes, Peppe thought. He wanted to see her dead, but not unhappy.

"Really?" the woman sneered. "He's hurt, is he?"

Peppe was about to say no, but the captain's hand on his arm stopped him.

"Does little Peppe not realize that he isn't paid to be sensitive?" she asked. Peppe didn't look at her because between being angry and trying not to laugh, he didn't know if he could speak.

"Yes, madam," the captain said.

"He's paid to do what he is told to do."

"Of course, madam," the captain said, smiling his sickly smile again. "He understands that."

"Good," the woman said, staring first at the captain, then at Peppe, then back at the captain. "That's clear then. I want a spicy grilled fuckin for dinner."

It was everything Peppe could do to spin and walk to the galley before bursting into laughter.

The captain was right behind him, a real smile on his face for the first time in days. He tossed the bag the woman had given him into the sink.

"What is that?" the chef asked.

"That's what they want you to cook for them tonight."

The chef peeked into the bag, opening it with one finger and then turning away. "I can't cook that. It's the most disgusting fishes man has ever seen, if it is fishes. Where did you get it?"

"She got it," Peppe said, still laughing, which caused the captain to laugh again. It was wonderful, to be able to make fun of such a woman.

"Cook Peppe's fishes," the captain said, waving away the bag in the sink. "Pretend it's their fishes. Who will know?"

The chef nodded and later that night, when the woman tasted Peppe's fish and said, "Now, how about that? That is what I call fish."

Peppe again had to retreat to the galley to keep from laughing right in her face.

7

AMBER LET THE SWEAT RUN DOWN HER FACE AND NECK as she worked the old exercise cycle as hard as she could. She had her exercises planned carefully. First she did a quick sprint, then a longer, smoother pace, then back to a quick sprint. That way she worked all the muscles and gave her heart and lungs a good workout as well.

The wind from the ship's movement gave her a little relief from the blazing hot sun, but not much. It was still before breakfast, and it was clear today was going to be the hottest day yet of the trip. She would need to watch her fluids and make sure she got some fruit juice when she was done exercising and before eating breakfast.

Beside her Marina sat in a sun chair. The least amount of her bikini covered her. For some reason Marina liked letting the sun bake her skin. This morning she had also taken three pills of strange color and chased them with gin, iced, with a lime.

Marina had kept herself in an almost constant state of intoxication since they had come on board. She said it took the edge off the boredom.

This morning Marina was already well started, working on her second glass of gin. She would more than likely be half smashed by the time breakfast was served. Amber didn't know how Marina could drink gin before breakfast, let alone take the pills with it. Just the thought twisted Amber's stomach.

Amber was using exercise to try to keep away the boredom, but it wasn't working.

"Don't you ever get tired of doing that, sweetie?" Marina asked as Amber slowed after a hard sprint. Marina then took another large gulp of her drink and barely got the glass back on the small side table beside her chair.

"What else is there to do?"

Marina shrugged and pointed at her glass with a smile.

Amber kept pedaling, staring at the ocean in front of the ship. It was smooth, with gentle rolling waves.

The men were still belowdeck getting ready for another day, and who knew where brain-dead Debi was. More than likely still in bed sleeping. For a small boat, it was amazing how the six of them could keep spread out. Except at night and at meals,

Tony had managed to pretty much do his own thing so far. That was fine by Amber; she loved Tony, but both of them had long since stopped liking each other. Money and convenience kept their marriage together.

A noise behind her made Amber slow down her exercise and look around. The captain emerged from the galley door and started toward the back of the boat, away from them.

"I know what we can do," Amber said, laughing and winking at Marina. "A game." Then louder she shouted, "Oh, *Captain!*"

The captain turned, the silly smile painted on his face as it always was. At some point Amber decided she was going to make that smile go away.

He came back to them and nodded. "Yes, madam? You asked for me?"

"We'll be discreet about this," Amber said, keeping her voice lower than she normally would. She slowed her pedaling and leaned toward the captain slightly, glancing at Marina. "We have a complaint."

"Do we?" Marina asked, clearly not keeping up in her almost drunken haze.

"Go ahead," the captain said, his voice also lower, his smile only half there.

"Marina will tell you about it," Amber said, speeding up her pace on the old exercise bike and glancing out over the blue water and shallow waves. She held that for a moment, then smiled past the captain at her friend.

Marina was clearly caught by surprise. She sat up, barely keeping her suit in place as she leaned toward the captain, playing along with the game Amber had started.

"You should all change T-shirts before breakfast."

Amber almost applauded. Perfect!

"Why?" the captain asked, staring at Marina.

"Emmm," Marina said, clearly trying to think of a reason why they should change T-shirts.

"Because your staff smells," Amber said, picking up on the idea.

The captain looked stunned and hurt, the painted-on smile almost gone now.

"Smell?"

"Smell," Amber said.

He glanced first at Amber, then back at Marina.

Amber nodded.

Marina nodded and sipped her drink, her half smile hidden by her glass.

"Really?" the captain asked, sounding more like a little boy than a big, burly man.

"Really," Amber said. "And I don't mean of roses, Captain. It's not hygienic."

"Stinky?" the captain asked.

Amber managed to not laugh, although Marina snorted part of her drink and then coughed.

"Yes, *stinky*, Captain," Amber said, pedaling harder.

The guy looked almost hurt as he nodded.

"Oh, and Captain," Amber said before he could turn away, "I want some grapefruit juice when I get off of this antique."

He nodded and headed into the galley.

Both Amber and Marina somehow managed to not explode in laughter until he was inside.

Peppe stood in the galley, amazed, listening as the captain told everyone that they had to change their T-shirts.

"Why?" the chef asked.

"Not you," the captain said, waving away the chef's question. "That woman, the boss's wife, wants all of the men around her to change their T-shirts."

"That makes no sense," Peppe said. He really didn't understand.

"A game," the captain said. "Another rich-person's game. Nothing more."

"That bitch," Peppe said, now understanding. "She wants to play stupid games, I'll play with her. I'll change my T-shirt all right."

He stormed out of the galley and down the hallway to the crew's quarters. He pulled a T-shirt out of his locker and looked at it, smiling. His old girlfriend had given it to him as a joke. On the chest was a picture of two cartoon characters fucking, but it was faint enough and decorative enough that you had to look pretty closely to see it.

He put on the T-shirt, glanced in the mirror and laughed, then went back to the galley.

"What are you doing?" the captain asked, seeing him come in. "Take that off. It's disgusting."

The chef laughed and shook his head, going back to mixing his batter.

"It's a fresh T-shirt and that's what signora I'm-a-motherfuckin'-bitch asked for. Give me the grapefruit juice."

The captain handed him the glass and Peppe headed out onto the deck. The bitch woman was toweling off, rubbing her legs. A few days ago that sight might have given him thoughts of other matters closer to the events portrayed in the picture on his shirt, but he was so angry at her, touching her now was the last thing on his mind. What he really wanted to do was take her and slap some sense into her.

"Grapefruit juice, madam," he said, handing it to her.

"Thank you," she said, staring at his T-shirt. Then she clearly saw the images. "Do you have children, Pee Pee, or just the mind of a child?"

"What?" Peppe asked, keeping his face straight.

She pointed at his chest. "That cartoon you're wearing."

Peppe looked down at his shirt, then back up at her, holding her gaze with as innocent an expression as he could muster. "You requested us to change our T-shirts, madam."

"That shirt offends me," she said, staring right at him, daring him to say anything.

He kept his mouth shut, so she went on. "It's revolting."

Again he said nothing. But saying nothing was hard, and not laughing even harder.

"Change it!" she ordered.

"Subtle," Marina said.

"Oh shut up, you drunk," Amber said.

Peppe just smiled at Amber, then turned and headed back into the galley, doing his best to not start laughing until he was far, far out of her earshot.

For most of the day Peppe had managed to avoid the woman. He had changed his shirt again, but her reaction to his cartoon shirt had put him in a good mood all day. And not having to wait on her helped keep it good.

He had simply fished near the back of the boat and stayed to himself as much as he could.

Now the stars were out in full, painting the sky with a silver brush. He loved it out on the open water, away from the lights, on a clear summer night such as this one. The air had cooled, but wasn't yet brisk. The sounds of the water lapping against the hull of the boat would calm even the most frayed nerves.

He had been standing, leaning against the rail, just staring out at the silver water and stars, for most of an hour before the captain came up beside him and sighed heavily.

"What are they up to now?" Peppe asked, not even looking at the captain.

"Strikes me dead," the captain said, clearly disgusted. "These rich people never fail to surprise me. The husbands have gone to bed, while the wives stay up playing cards and drinking."

Peppe just shook his head. That wasn't the way things worked where he was from.

"What kind of husbands are they? They got everything the wrong way around."

"Yeah," the captain said, "stupid, huh?"

The captain glanced around, as if making sure no one was close by. Peppe did the same, not knowing why. The closest person was another sailor on the bow. No one else was on deck.

The captain took out something from his pocket and held it for Peppe to see. "Look what I found in the brunette's cabin. I think it's cocaine."

Peppe looked at the bag of white powder in the

captain's hand. He didn't want to ask the captain what he was doing snooping around the brunette's cabin. It was his boat and the captain could go where he wanted, Peppe figured.

"Cocaine?" Peppe asked, interested.

Peppe held the bag out away from his face. "I bet it's something Professor Drug-You-Up made in his laboratory. It probably flies you to the moon in a couple of minutes."

"Want to try it?" the captain asked, staring at the joint in his hand. "I have never been to the moon."

Peppe looked at the big man, stunned. "You are the captain. What chance do we have of making it to Italy if you want to go to the moon?"

Peppe had been on a couple of ships over the years where the captain was either drinking or taking drugs. That was the last thing they all needed on this trip.

"Come on," the captain said, holding up the joint in his hand and looking at it in the starlight. "Let's try it. What's the worst that can happen?"

Peppe had images of this captain acting like the other captains he had known who were too far gone on drugs to ever be allowed to board a ship. "You could get hooked, go mad, get sick, swat flies that aren't there, take things that don't belong to you, and go to jail. I know, I've seen it all happen."

"Just a little?" the captain asked, almost whining.

Peppe faced the big man. "What's wrong with you?"

The man looked sullen.

"Go to bed and I'll forget you lost control."

"Fuck you," the captain said, now angry. "We could have gone to the moon, maybe had an orgy."

Peppe laughed at the captain's imagination. "I don't want to have an orgy with you, Captain. Go to bed, you idiot."

The captain spun on his heels and stormed toward the door leading to his quarters.

"You've lost your mind just thinking about taking that," Peppe shouted after him.

The captain slammed the door, the sound echoing over the calm ocean.

Peppe stepped back into the shadows along the rail, waiting, listening. He wanted to make sure the captain was completely gone. Finally, when the boat seemed as calm as it had before the captain showed up, Peppe took the bag in his hand.

Then, suddenly, the bag slipped from his fingers. He tried to catch it, but it dropped to the black water below.

"Damn," he said. "What a waste."

"I'm going out for air," Amber said.

Peppe stepped back into the shadows even more, but he knew that there was far too much light out tonight for her to miss him.

She came out on the deck wearing a halter dress.

Her blond hair was swept off her face; her tanned arms and legs gleamed in the starlight.

She moved to the rail and faced forward, letting the ship's breeze run through her hair.

In the starlight, on the deck of this ship in the middle of the water, she would be considered beautiful. Under any normal circumstances, he would be attracted to her.

She stretched, showing him her fine body from behind as she worked out the looseness in her muscles by twisting first to one side, then to the other.

As long as she didn't speak, he could watch her and enjoy the sight.

Suddenly she turned around, as if she had sensed him there, staring at her.

She looked him right in the eye, as if actually seeing him.

At that moment, as their gazes held, he would have sworn she was actually attracted to him, actually was afraid of him.

Then she broke the gaze and, without saying a word, went through the door and below deck.

She had been just a woman tonight, not spoiling the moment by speaking. Peppe had no doubt that if she would learn to do that more often, she would make her husband a far happier man.

8

THE SUN WAS LOW ON THE HORIZON BUT STILL A GOOD distance above the waves as Amber climbed up on deck and into the remaining heat of the day. She had been sleeping, fitfully, and had awoken to silence. No laughter, no arguing, nothing. For a moment she thought everyone had gone off and left her alone on the boat in the middle of the ocean. The thought sent waves of panic through her.

She put on a black bikini and went quickly up on deck. As she got into the sun she saw two crewmen cleaning the engine.

She stopped in the doorway and let herself take a deep breath, calming her racing heart as much as she could. The normal workings of the crew relieved her fear.

As she watched, another crewman joined the other two. The ship was hardly moving through the water, leaving no real wind to cool the hot, humid evening. Off to one side was a rock-faced island that looked more like a pile of dog shit sitting on the blue water than anything else.

Again she was faced with the same problem she had been facing since they got on board this old bucket of bolts. There was nothing to do. A person could only do so much eating, drinking, sitting in the sun, and riding an exercise bike before going stark raving nuts.

"I am bored," she said, yawning, as she walked up to where the captain stood watching his men work. "What time is it?"

"Seven P.M. madam," he said, not looking at her.

"Seven P.M.?" she asked. She was surprised. It was later than she had expected, yet dinner was a while off. That left her with nothing to do for almost two hours.

"Yes, madam," the captain said, this time turning and smiling at her.

"Where is everyone?" she asked.

The captain indicated Marina, who was stretched out on a chaise in the aft section of the ship, near one of the sailors working on the engine. She was clearly flirting with him.

"The rest took a dinghy to the caves on the other side of the island." The captain pointed at the brown lump sticking out of the water. To Amber it looked just like any of the other hundred islands they had passed.

Earlier in the day the captain had been talking to Tony about the caves they would pass by, and how wonderful they were to explore. She hadn't listened to most of the talk, since she had no real intention of going inside some dark cave on a remote island in the middle of nowhere.

She looked around, then spotted Peppe, who was fishing off the back of the boat, hunched over the rail as if he was hiding from everything going on. Just seeing him standing there twisted her stomach. Her attraction for him had turned to hate and anger, and she wasn't sure why. All she knew was that on this boring trip, the most enjoyment she was getting was from making Peppe angry. And she had to admit, that wasn't hard to do.

Suddenly an idea caught her. With two hours until the scheduled dinner, there would be time to go to the caves and make sure the others got back in time. The little trip would keep her busy and break some of the boredom. And maybe along the way she could figure out a way to get under Peppe's skin one more time. It wasn't much of a sport, but on a trip this boring, it was all she had.

"Guido," she shouted, purposely mangling the hairy Italian's name just like she always did, "lower the second dinghy. I want to go to see the cave."

Peppe turned from his fishing and looked at her, clearly shocked. She smiled at him, happy that she had caught him off guard.

"Madam," the captain said, "they should be returning soon."

"I want to make sure of that," she said, waving away his comment.

"Marina?" she said, moving away from the captain toward the second dinghy. "You coming?"

Marina winked at the crewman she had been flirting with. "I think I have overcooked it a little this afternoon, sweetie," she said. She never looked at Amber, but instead kept her gaze on the bare-chested crewman. "I'll think I'll stay right here."

Amber had no doubt that if Marina could manage it, she would drag that sailor off into some hidden compartment before Michael got back. Besides drinking, sex with strangers was Marina's way of breaking any kind of boredom, both here and back home.

"Madam," Peppe said, coming up behind her. "It's too late."

She turned and stared into his deep eyes. "I'll be the judge of that, thank you."

She headed toward where the second dinghy was hanging off the edge of the boat, ready to be lowered.

"Don't get cold, sweetie," Marina said, again never taking her gaze from the sweat-covered man.

What Marina saw in such lowlifes Amber would never know. To Amber, the only fun with someone like that was holding them in their position. And making them angry. Playing with them like she played with Peppe.

She glanced around at where Peppe stood, not moving. "So what's going on with the dinghy?"

"Madam," Peppe said, shaking his head, "there's a current, and the wind is wrong."

"So what?" Amber asked, feeling the anger build. Why couldn't this man just do as he was told? Why was everything always so difficult with him?

Peppe pointed out over the water at the edge of the island. "Just that the caves aren't close," he said, "and the sun is near setting. The others will be back within the hour. My advice to you is that you shouldn't go."

"Oh, really?" Amber said, now really angry. How dare this scum of a sailor tell her what she should and shouldn't do. "Well, my advice to you is that you should get the fuckin' dinghy down and get ready."

She spun and stared at the captain, who only shrugged at Peppe.

She turned back and smiled as the hairy Italian shook his head and began working to lower the dinghy in to the ocean. As long as he kept fighting her on this trip, she wouldn't be bored.

* * *

There was no doubt in Peppe's mind that making this trip was a very bad idea. And not just because he was going be alone with that woman for thirty minutes, but because there was a storm coming. He had sensed it earlier; now he knew it. As they pulled away from the boat, he could see that the waves were starting to swell higher, caps at the tops. They banged into the dinghy like fists hitting a sad, old boxer.

On the shore of the island the waves pounded the rocks as if they were angry at the stone for getting in the way. Water spewed upward in foam and mist, and the sound of the surf was slowly increasing to a pounding roar that could be both felt and heard over the sound of the engine.

This craft wasn't the best, most stable thing Peppe had ever been on. Not the worst, but far from the best, and the engine had already sputtered twice in the first two minutes, threatening to quit at any moment.

The engine had done that the other day as well, and Peppe had complained to the captain about the motor. The man had just shrugged and said he would check it out when they got finished with this trip.

The blond woman sat on the front side of the dinghy, facing him, hanging on to the side with white knuckles. She had clearly not expected the ocean to be this rough. Maybe it would teach her to listen to people who knew what they were talking about.

He laughed at his own stupid thought, the sound snapped off by the growing wind. Nothing would teach that woman anything beyond her own spoiled, selfish thoughts.

Peppe glanced around. The boat had disappeared as they went around the first edge of the island. The caves were still a distance around the rock cliffs. Peppe had been here twice before and never understood why tourists liked the caves. They were nothing more than wide holes in the rocks that boats could float up inside. There were a few old rocks from a past when someone built some sort of protection inside one of the caves. And there was a sand beach in another. Nothing more.

The current on this side of the island was shoving them away from the rocks, making the going slow. He had to keep adjusting for the drift to the right.

Peppe kept hoping that they would meet the other dinghy coming back, but so far there had been no sign. More than likely if they had gone this way around the island to get to the caves they would go the other way around to get back to the boat. That was just normal tourist sightseeing thinking.

He glanced up at the darkening sky and the clouds that seemed to be racing by overhead. If they didn't turn back soon, they might be spending the night in the caves for shelter. The thought of having to spend the night with this woman, trapped in a damp cave, was not his idea of a good time.

In fact, it was his worst nightmare.

"Why is that thing strapped to the engine?" the woman asked, just loud enough so that he could hear her over the sounds of the motor.

Peppe glanced down at the engine just as the spray from a wave hit it, causing it to sputter again. "That's my Saint Christopher," Peppe said. "Patron saint for travelers. I never go anywhere without it." He had put it there when he lowered the dinghy into the water.

"How touching," Amber said, shaking her head and looking off at the island rocks and the waves pounding them.

He didn't care what she thought of his St. Christopher. At the moment, they were going to need the saint's help to make it back to the boat before this storm got worse.

"Listen, madam," he said, "it's all the same to me, but I must warn you it's getting dark soon."

He watched as the woman, wearing dark sunglasses, glanced up at the sky. He knew she had no idea at all what she was looking at, if she could even see with those glasses on as the light dimmed. Maybe she was just used to walking around in the dark, ordering other people around, never seeing anything real.

"We'll manage," she said.

"I've warned you," he said, his voice as cold and as calm as he could make it.

She glanced at him, but he couldn't see what she was feeling behind the glasses.

"Jesus, man," she said, holding on as another larger wave banged into their craft, "what's wrong with you? Are you scared or something?"

"Scared?" Peppe asked, his voice low and cold. Again this bitch of a woman had managed to get him angry. "I am a fisherman. I was conceived on the crest of a wave and born in the belly of a boat. What is the meaning of this word 'scared,' madam?"

At that moment what he had been worried about happened. A large wave slapped into the rubber dinghy, rocking it and sending spray up and over the side of the craft, splashing the engine.

The motor sputtered twice and then stopped, plunging them into the silence of a wide ocean, broken only by the wind and the surf against the island's rocks.

"I knew it, I knew it," he said in Italian, turning to the outboard motor. He reset the starter on the old machine and pulled the starter cord as hard as he could. Nothing.

He reset it and tried again.

Nothing.

"Another joke, nature boy?" Amber asked, her

voice now loud in the wind and silence of the ocean surface. The sound of the surf pounding against the island rocks was now much louder. It was lucky for them the current was pushing them away from those sharp things.

He shook his head and answered without looking back at her. "It's the engine, not me," he said. "It's old and a little touchy."

He bent over to make sure the air intake vents had not been clogged, then banged the engine hard on the side to try to break free anything that might be causing the problem, then tried to start it again.

Nothing.

"I can show you touchy, Guido," the woman said. "I said start the engine."

Peppe's anger boiled up. He turned and faced her, doing his best to not lash out at her. It would be so easy just to dump her overboard and be done with the bitch. The world would thank him, he was sure. But instead he just stared at her.

"I said start the engine," she repeated.

Her glaring eyes seemed to cut right through him, but he glared right back, not giving her an inch.

"Number one," he said, "my name is Peppe, not Guido or Pee Pee. Please get it right."

He waited for a second, then went on. "Number two, I can't start an engine that doesn't want to be started."

He turned back to the motor, trying to control his anger. "Filthy slut! Dirty whore," he said in Italian. "What does she think I'm doing?"

"If you don't mind, let's stick to one language."

He banged the engine with his fist one more time, wishing it was her head instead, then checked the starter, and pulled on the starter cord again.

It turned over, sputtered, and stopped.

Once more.

Nothing.

"If we could see the others, at least I wouldn't mind so much," she said.

He glanced back at her as she searched the island shoreline.

He knew that unless they got very lucky no one was going to see them. They were on the wrong side of the island from the boat, and the current was shoving them away. Their only choice was to get the engine running before the wind and current took them too far off course.

"What's the matter?" he asked. "You scared?"

"How scared do I look?" she asked, staring right at him.

Peppe shook his head and turned back to the engine. "I could take the engine that runs your mouth," he whispered, just soft enough that she couldn't hear him. "We wouldn't have any problems then."

He bent down under the motor and unscrewed the

engine cap, then took it off, placing it to one side on the seat of the dinghy. At first glance he couldn't see anything wrong. The wires seemed to be tight, nothing was burnt-looking, no fuel was leaking, no hoses out of place.

"Is it broken?" she asked.

"No," he said, "it's never worked better." He waved his hand at the darkening open sea around them. "See how we glide across the waves."

He looked her straight in the eye. "Tell me, am I going too fast, madam?"

"You're going fast enough for a slap in the face, Mr. Born-on-the-crest-of-a-wave."

"No, no," he said, shaking his head at her and smiling. "I was conceived on the crest of a wave and born in the belly of a boat. Please get it right."

She shrugged. "Whatever. Are you sure we have gas?"

"Yes, yes," he said, kicking the gas tank. "We have gas for almost two hours."

He turned back to the engine, checked a few more wires and lines for tightness, then grabbed the pullcord starter and yanked.

Nothing.

He tried again.

Nothing. It wasn't even sputtering now.

"Enough of all the theatrics, Captain Conception-in-the-bowels-of-a-boat."

He banged the engine with his fist one more time and then tried pulling on the pull-cord starter three fast times.

Nothing.

He dropped back on his seat, knocking the engine cap into the bottom of the dinghy at her feet.

"Leave it alone," she said, "before you do me some harm."

"And what do you suggest we do?" he asked.

"We wait for the others to come by," she said. "I am sure they won't be long."

He started to remind her about the wind and the currents, then thought better of it. There was no doubt that if the other boat didn't come by within the next few minutes, the wind and current was going to take them far enough away from the island that they might not be seen. Especially with the growing size of the swells and the fading light.

He was going to have to be very lucky to escape being stuck on this boat with this woman for the rest of the night. What had he done to deserve this sort of hell?

9

THE DARKNESS CAME FAST, AS IT ALWAYS DID OVER THE ocean. The clouds were blocking out the stars, making the water around the dinghy look black and dangerous.

Peppe could see that the swells had risen at least two feet since they had left the boat, and now were tall enough that he couldn't see over the crests when they were in the trough of the waves.

He had done as she had asked and not bothered with the engine for a few minutes, just sitting and waiting. But it was clear to him that the others had taken a different route around the island back to the boat. With the wind and the currents, even the island was fading in the distance.

So he went back to work on the engine, doing his best to check everything in the growing darkness.

"I should have gotten the captain to take me," Amber said. "I bet he could have fixed it."

Peppe glanced around at her. She was sitting, hands under her chin, looking bored.

"Why don't you go and get him?" Peppe asked, going back to work on the old motor.

She didn't answer.

There was nothing he could see that was wrong with the engine. It should start; it should be running. He stood, braced himself against the wooden seat, and yanked on the pull cord as hard as he could.

Nothing.

He kept yanking, trying to get the engine to kick over.

No luck at all. The engine just didn't want to work for some reason that he couldn't see in the darkness.

"Aren't we going too far out?" Amber asked, staring at the island.

Peppe sat down on the wooden bench, breathing hard from all the exercise, and glanced at the now clearly smaller island vanishing quickly in the darkness. "I warned you about the wind and current."

"My God," she said. "Why go out in a boat if you can't operate it?"

He just stared at her, keeping his anger in check. There wasn't going to be much point in making her any angrier than she already was, since he had no doubt they were going to be stuck together for the night.

"What kind of fuckin' sailor are you?" she demanded.

He said nothing. Luckily she hadn't noticed the oars yet in the bottom of the boat. She would have him rowing all night, and there was no way he could row faster than the wind and current was moving them.

"Give me your sweater." She grabbed it from the seat where he had tossed it before they started. He had learned very early on to never go anywhere in a boat without extra clothing.

She sniffed it and tossed it back on the bench. "Jesus, what have you been doing in that?"

"I am a fisherman," Peppe said. "Not a sailor. Because I am a fisherman, I go fishing in it, so it smells of fishes."

She turned away from him, clearly shivering, staring out over the water in the now almost total darkness.

Peppe thought about trying to work even more on the engine, then realized that in the dark all he might do is make it worse. He sat back against the rubber side of the dinghy, trying as much as possible to get out of the wind that seemed to be growing colder by the second.

"It's pitch black," she said. "How are they going to see us?"

Peppe shook his head at the stupidity of the woman.

"If they were coming, they would have passed us by now. They might have decided to go the other way around the island."

"Oh, come on," she said, turning to look at him.

He could see just enough of her face in the dim light to tell she was losing all her control. Fear was starting to take her, and that would do neither of them any good.

"This isn't funny anymore," she said. "I want to go back to the yacht."

She sounded like the spoiled child she was. Faced with an unpleasant situation, all she could do was stamp her foot and demand attention. Peppe found it disgusting.

"It's a yacht now, is it?" Peppe said, shaking his head. "You are not getting this, are you? We can't go back just because you want us to. We have to get rescued, or fix the engine."

"Well, fix the fuckin' thing," she shouted, the panic now clear in her voice. She pointed at the engine cover. "Or get the patron saint of travelers there to fix it."

Peppe glanced at his St. Christopher medal still connected to the engine cover. "We will always be safe while he is there."

"Aren't there any oars?" Amber asked, digging at the bottom of the boat in the darkness.

"Yes," Peppe said, sighing. He had hoped she

wouldn't see those yet. "But which way are you going to row?"

Amber and Peppe both looked out over the ocean. At the crest of the waves all he could see was blackness and a the faint light of the horizon as the last of the sun vanished. He knew in which direction the boat was, but he also knew that no amount of rowing against this current and wind would get them there.

He was stuck for the night with the nastiest, most spoiled woman he had ever met. Maybe even longer than one night, depending on how far the winds and current took them and how soon someone would find them. He didn't mind so much being lost at sea. He knew he could survive that.

But surviving in this boat with her might be another matter entirely.

Amber could not remember being this cold before. Where had the heat of the day gone?

An hour ago she had finally gotten over the smell and put on Peppe's sweater. The fish odor had choked her, but at least the sweater gave some warmth, even though it smelled like a fish market in San Francisco. She would have to take a long, hot shower when this was over just to get the smell off of her skin.

She was sitting on the bottom of the boat, trying to stay below the cold wind.

Peppe was sitting in the back, also on the floor, clearly shivering. With her wearing his sweater, all he had on was his T-shirt. But it served him right for getting her into this mess. Maybe next time he'd know better. She just couldn't believe how stupid this hairy Italian was.

"Look at this," she said. "I'm stuck on a raft in the middle of the ocean with a fuck-wit of a seaman for comfort."

"Please, madam," he said, not looking at her, "don't use language like that."

"Why not?" she demanded. "Are you feeling a little *sensitive* tonight?"

"It's just not polite," he said.

God, she was beginning to really hate this guy. How she had ever had any attraction to him in the first place was beyond her. Now all he did was make her angry.

"Well, it's not polite you putting me on this fuckin' little dinghy and breaking down in the middle of the antfuckin'arctic, now is it?"

She watched as he shook his head and kept his gaze straight forward over the rubber edge of the raft. "I told you it wasn't a good idea, madam."

"You didn't tell me the engine might break down, did you?" she demanded. "Why don't you radio someone, or send a flare off?"

Again he just shook his head. She could tell he

clearly thought her stupid. How could anyone who was a common seaman and put medals on engines for good luck think her stupid?

She leaned over and yanked off the St. Christopher medal from the engine cover still on the floor of the raft between them. Then, before he could stop her, she tossed it over the side into the black ocean.

"And what good has he done us?"

Peppe sat staring out over the edge of the raft for a moment, then turned and looked directly at her. Even in the near darkness, she could tell he was as angry as she could ever imagine a man being at her.

She scooted back away from him.

"What have you done?" he said, his voice low and cold and mean. Then he said something just as nasty-sounding in Italian and turned away from her.

She sat there, huddled in the bottom of the boat, not daring to say anything, as the waves shoved the dinghy around. She knew that she had crossed a line with him. She knew she had pushed him too far. Now all she could do was just sit and wait and hope they made it through the night.

She had no doubt it was going to be a long, cold night, the longest she had ever lived through.

10

Peppe came up out of sleep like swimming to the surface of a murky lake. The light around him was bright and warm, making him squint until he remembered where he was.

He had been dreaming of a woman who turned into a giant snake. He had been attracted to the snake, had kissed the snake, had been swallowed by the snake, and then spit out, only to start the process all over.

Never, in his memory, had he had a worse nightmare.

He opened his eyes, shading them from the bright sun, slowly remembering more and more about last night, realizing awake he was still in the middle of a nightmare almost as bad as the one he had dreamed.

Around him there was nothing but calm, blue water. Not one glimpse of land of any kind.

Amber, the snake woman from his dream, slept curled against the rubber side of the dinghy. Her face was peaceful, almost beautiful in the morning light. If she didn't have such a hateful personality, his attraction for her might still be alive.

If she were nicer, being with her on this raft might be an adventure instead of something to dread worse than a bad disease. He couldn't believe he was trapped with a spoiled bitch like her in the middle of the ocean. It was the worst thing he could ever have imagined happening.

Being eaten by a snake would be better, of that he had no doubt.

He reached down over the edge of the dinghy and splashed water on his face, being careful to not let any of it get in his mouth or eyes. The feel of the cool water pushed the memory of the dream a little farther away.

He stood and stripped off his T-shirt and rolled up the legs of his pants. It was going to be a very hot day on the water. There was no point in wearing any more than he needed to.

He reached into his pocket and pulled out his penknife, then with a disgusted look at the still-sleeping woman, he bent down and started to work on the engine. He knew that something had to be causing the engine to stop. All he had to do was find it.

He had no idea what they would do if he got the

engine started, but at least they would have it as an option if they needed it.

"Look at the mess I'm in," he said softly to himself in Italian as he studied the motor to figure out what to try first. "All because of that bitch. Why did it have to be me?"

He used the knife to unscrew a gas-line hose and check it for clogs. Then he put it back in place and started to work on another hose.

As he worked to take out one screw the knife got stuck, jammed down between a clamp and the engine block. He tried to work it free, but it stayed stuck until, using all his force, he yanked it out.

The knife slid out of his hands, flipped end over end, bounced once on the side of the dinghy, and splashed into the water. If he lost that knife there would be no way to fix the engine or cut fish if he caught any.

He went over the side in a smooth dive, following the knife down into the clear water, not giving a second thought to anything but getting that knife back.

He caught it about ten meters down, put the knife in his mouth, turned and kicked for the bright surface and the dark shape of the bottom of the boat over him like a cloud on a clear day.

He surfaced right near the engine, at the back, only to hear shouting.

"Peppe!"

Peppe laughed to himself and said nothing, keeping himself near the back of the boat and out of sight. So she did know his name after all.

"Giuseppe!" she shouted, her voice disappearing out over the smooth, open sea. "Giuseppe! Help! Oh, God!"

She knew his full name. Even more interesting.

The sound of panic in her voice changed to screaming. He shook his head at how worthless one person could be. He dove down under the boat and popped up beside the craft, quickly pulling himself back in the boat.

The moment she saw him she stopped screaming.

He took the knife out of his mouth and smiled at her. "You miss me?"

Amber looked confused for a second, then said, "I wanted to know if there was a storm coming."

Peppe looked around. There wasn't a cloud anywhere to be seen. Nothing but crystal-blue sky merging down into deep blue ocean.

He said nothing. Anything he did say would just make her mad.

The silence between them grew until it seemed like the entire world might break open from the brittleness.

"What happened to the island?" Amber finally asked, clearly still breathing hard from her episode of missing him.

He cleared the salt from his nose over the edge and didn't answer her.

"What are those idiots doing?" she asked, turning around a few times, searching the horizon. "Why haven't they come? What have they been doing all night?"

Peppe wanted to say that they were more than likely celebrating that she was gone, but he didn't. Instead he said, "The sea is a big place. It might take a while."

He managed to pry off the hose he'd been working on when he dropped the knife, blew through it to clean it, and then started putting it back in position.

"A while?" Amber asked, standing up on the bench. She started to do some stretching exercises, the same ones she had done every morning back on the yacht. "What's a while?"

With a glance back, he said, "The tourist season is over. There are not many boats around. So I don't know, maybe a couple of weeks."

Peppe could sense that she had stopped moving behind him. He could almost feel the intensity of her gaze as it bore into his back while he worked on the engine.

"A couple of *weeks?*"

The panic was back in her voice again.

He laughed, not looking at her. "I was joking. Maybe a couple of days."

"Very fuckin' funny," she said. "If you think I am going to spend another hour, let alone a couple of days, on this dinghy with you, you are mistaken."

Peppe shrugged as he finished replacing the tube. "Oh well, get off then."

He stood, put the knife back in his pocket, checked the engine one more time, and then yanked on the pull-cord starter.

"Where is God when you need him?" Amber asked.

Peppe yanked again on the cord, not telling her that he doubted God had bothered to listen to her complaining and foul mouth for years.

"What about charts, choppers, radar, computers?" she said, clearly ranting. "Call the Marines, bribe a fuckin' dolphin. Just get me off this fuckin' bath toy."

Peppe had no idea who exactly she was talking to. He yanked on the cord three times in quick succession. He could feel a difference, as if the engine was about to kick over and start.

"Stop fuckin' around with that thing pretending you know something about it!" she shouted at him.

He ignored her.

He braced himself on the wooden seat and then, using all his strength, he yanked on the starter cord. The force of his movement rocked the boat and knocked Amber off the front bench where she had been standing, sending her down to the floor of the dinghy with a loud *oomph*.

The engine sputtered twice and then started, filling the air and silent ocean around them with the wonderful sound. Blue smoke puffed from the back of the motor for a few seconds, then drifted lazily out over the water as the engine settled down into a steady rhythm.

He made sure the throttle was set right, then turned and smiled at her. "What was that you were saying?"

"There *is* a God!" she shouted, scrambling back up on the wooden bench. "I am converted. I asked and I received. It was me He listened to."

"Of course He did," Peppe said, not daring to say anything else he was thinking.

She stared at him for a long second, then said, "Enough of your smart mouth and smart ass. Get me out of this."

"Which way, please?" Peppe said, waving his arm at the expanse of open sea around them.

"Why are you asking me?"

Peppe shrugged. "I won't accept the responsibility."

Nothing she could say would make him. If he did pick a direction, she would be harping at him within ten minutes. He had a very rough idea where they had come from because of his knowledge of the currents and the position of the sun, but only rough. Not enough to find a small yacht on a large ocean.

They were better off drifting and letting someone else find them. He just wanted to get the motor running in case they did drift close enough to land to use it.

"Come on," she said. "You're the sailor."

"That's not what you said last night."

"That was last night," she said, waving away his comment as if swatting a pesky bug hovering around her face. "Now take me home."

"I am a fisherman, not a sailor," he said, staring at her. "You tell me."

She stared at him as if he were a bug to be squashed. "Well, fishermen know about the sea. You said you were born in the fuckin' thing. Jesus, man, figure it out."

"How?" Peppe said.

The anger was back in her voice now. "Use the stars or something."

Peppe looked up at the sky, pretending to look for stars in the bright blue expanse. "Ahh, the stars. That's a good idea, madam."

"Listen, Pee Pee," she said, the anger now not hidden. Her eyes were slitted, her breath coming hard and fast. "I have had enough of your back talk. You are the employee. I am the employer."

Peppe wanted to say she was much more than that, but didn't. Instead he just stared at her and asked, "Which way then, *employer*?"

"Just get me to land and I won't mention how abusive you have been during this painful and traumatic experience."

He shook his head in disgust, turned, and engaged the engine. If she wanted to be taken somewhere, then he would take her. But he knew it would do no good and only waste their gas.

She scrambled to sit down and hold on as the boat kicked up speed over the smooth surface, running as though nothing had ever happened. Whatever he had done had fixed the engine's problem, for the moment at least.

"Which way are we going?" she asked, glancing back at him as her blond hair blew in her face.

"You tell me," he said. "Do you prefer left or right?"

"Enough of your jokes," she said, staring at him.

"There is no joking matter, madam," he said. "You want to go left? I'll go left."

He turned the engine and the boat swerved left.

"Right, we can go right?"

He turned the boat hard right.

Both times she had to hang on to keep from getting tossed against the side of the dinghy.

"You'll regret this, nature boy," she said.

"Maybe," he said, shrugging, "but I refuse to accept responsibility. Tell me where you want to go. Do you want to stop and sunbathe?"

He let the boat slow and stop. It rocked gently in

its own wave. He then sat there, waiting for her directions, a stern look on his face.

Somehow, she managed to not scream at him, but he wasn't sure how, considering how angry she looked.

Two hours later the boat ran out of gas. There was still no land in sight in any direction.

11

THE GENTLE WAVES CARESSED PEPPE'S FACE LIKE A woman's soft hand as he leaned over the side of the dinghy. He had dug out a snorkel and mask from the tourist supplies in the dinghy and now had his face in the water, watching a small school of sardines flitting back and forth in the shade of the raft.

"You should have gone straight," Amber said behind him.

He ignored her, as he had been doing since she had forced him to run the dinghy's engine out of gas. It was the stupidest thing he had ever been forced to do. More than likely, by running for two hours, they had just put themselves farther out of reach of rescue.

And now starving was going to become an issue, right after getting water. He couldn't do anything about the water, but he might be able to keep them from starving, and get a little moisture in their bodies at the same time.

Under this hot sun, without protection and fresh water, they would be lucky to last three days.

The school of sardines moved closer to him as the raft turned slightly, changing the shape of the shade under it. "Come here," he said to the fish in Italian. "Come to Daddy."

He had one hand open in the water, holding it still, waiting. He was a fisherman. He knew how to be patient, wait for the fishes to come to him.

The fish swarmed around his arm and hand, thinking it nothing more than part of the raft.

He felt them flutter against the palm of his hand. As quick as he could he closed his fist. He had missed a good dozen times before, but this time his fist closed around a finger-long sardine.

He pushed himself up out of the water and back on the bench in the boat, pulling off the mask to look at the fish. It was a beautiful little thing. Then, before it could wiggle free from his grasp, he bit its head off.

He could feel the crunch of the spine and a few squirts of liquid as his mouth filled with the taste of sardine.

He spit the head out over the side.

"Jesus," Amber said, a look of disgust on her face, "what are you doing?"

"I am trying to save us from dying of thirst and hunger," he said.

He held out the sardine to Amber.

She stared at it as if it were an alien creature. "What?"

"Eat part of it. Take a bite."

"That?!" she said, her voice full of complete disgust.

"Can't you wrap in up in some rice or something?"

Peppe just shook his head. The woman was serious. In all his days he had never met someone so lost to any reality. If that was what having money did to a person, he wanted to stay poor all his life.

"Here's a bit of salt," he said, dipping the fish in the water, then offering it to her. "How's that?"

He put the sardine down in front of her on the bench, then went to get the mask to try for another one.

"Go ahead," he said, picking up the mask and washing it out in the water.

Slowly she picked up the fish between her thumb and finger, as if it might bite her. She sniffed it, wrinkling her nose. Then she summoned up the courage to take a tiny bite.

"Yuk!" she said, spitting. "It's disgusting."

She whipped around and threw it into the sea.

Peppe stared at her, stunned. Stupidity seemed to

be a disease with this woman. Terminal for both of them if he didn't watch out.

"Why did you do that?" he demanded. "I could have eaten it myself. It took me hours to catch it with my own bare hands and you threw it *away!*"

His voice got louder and more angry with every word. He desperately wanted to just slap her across the face. If there was a person in the world who deserved slapping, it was this woman.

"All right, calm down, little boy," she said as she dipped a cloth in the ocean and put it over her forehead. "You're embarrassing yourself. Fasting never hurt anybody."

"Are you serious?" Peppe asked.

She said nothing. Just closed her eyes and leaned back with the cloth on her head.

"We are *not* fasting," Peppe said, "we are starving. There is a big fuckin' difference. Starving has killed more people than dying of old age."

"Don't you swear at me," she said, opening her eyes and looking at him.

He was about to explode at her, screaming every swear word he could think of in Italian and English. But she didn't give him a chance.

She jumped up, pointing over his shoulder. "Oh, God, good God! Good God! Help!"

She was screaming at the top of her lungs by the time he turned around to see the big tourist ship. It was a good distance away, and unless someone standing at the rail with great eyesight happened to be looking directly at them, they were too far away to be seen. Too bad they didn't have any gas left for the engine. He might have been able to get them close enough to be rescued. By the time he rowed over there, the ship would be long gone.

He pulled a whistle out of the survival bag left in every dinghy and started blowing.

She turned, grabbed the whistle from him, and started blowing on it, not making half the noise that he could make. But she didn't seem to notice. She just stood there on the bench, blowing, flapping her arms like a wounded bird trying to fly.

Then she started jumping up and down while waving, as if getting a few inches higher in to the air would help the people on the big boat see them.

Every time she landed on the seat the dinghy tipped to one side or the other.

Peppe just stood, keeping his balance, and watched, shaking his head at the stupidity of the woman.

With one jump she tipped their boat enough that she lost her balance and fell against the rubber side. The whistle bounced out of her mouth and dropped into the water.

"She's thrown away my whistle," Peppe said in Italian.

Amber climbed back to her feet and continued to wave and shout.

"Help! We're shipwrecked. Help!"

Behind her Peppe raised his arm to just smack her across the side of her head. She was the stupidest human that had ever walked, and he desperately wanted to try knock some sense into her.

He held that position for a moment, then sat down, letting her go on shouting and jumping up and down.

After a few moments she looked around at him. "Why aren't you helping?" she demanded breathlessly.

"They'll never hear us," he said. "We're downwind of them, and too far away."

As always, she didn't listen.

"Then I'll get their attention," she said. She went back to screaming and shouting for help while waving her arms and jumping up and down.

Ten minutes later she collapsed in tears as the ship slowly moved away. Even he didn't have the heart to tell her that if she hadn't made him run the engine out of gas, they would have been rescued by now.

Amber could not believe that the ship hadn't seen them. She couldn't remember a time when she had been so excited, then so discouraged. For the first time since the hairy Italian had warned her about this taking days to get rescued, she was believing him. If he just hadn't let the engine run out of gas, they would have been rescued. How could a sailor be so stupid on the sea?

The rest of the day, after the ship passed, had gone by as slow as any day she could remember living. The sun had seemed hotter than before, and hunger was hurting her insides, causing her pains worse than cramps.

By the middle of the afternoon, lying on a baking hot raft on a calm ocean, she couldn't imagine how things could get any worse. But they did.

And as the evening got close, clouds covered the sunset, spinning past faster than she had ever thought clouds could move. The sea had gotten rougher than when they started last night. At one point she had asked Peppe if there was any way to keep the dinghy from rocking.

All he had done was laugh.

In fact, laughing at her was all he had done all day. He would pay for that when they got off this stupid raft, she would make sure of that.

By dark the rain had started, making her colder than the night before, and soaking everything. Her sunburned skin was extra sensitive to the pounding, cold water. Each drop felt as if someone was flicking her with a finger. Finally she had taken his fish-smelling jacket and put it over her head like a tent as she huddled against the rubber side of the boat. Every minute had seemed like an hour, and she was sure she wasn't going to make it through the night.

As the rain started, Peppe had caught a bunch of the water in a container in the survival kit and forced her to drink. She had to admit that even with the metal odor from the container, the water tasted better than anything she had drunk in a long time. She didn't tell him that.

Of course, he forced her to drink far too much, and now her stomach was hurting even worse. Were there any more ways this filthy man could punish her for being rich? She was sure he would think of them.

He took a long drink and then put out a number of other containers on his bench to catch even more water. She didn't know why he did that since there was going to be more than enough water in the bottom of the dinghy very shortly.

Amber used his jacket to cover her head, but with the bottom of the boat filling around her legs, she was losing feeling in her toes. After a few more minutes she pulled her knees up to her chin, keeping her feet on the bench.

He took another long drink and smiled at her. "At least we're not going to die of thirst for a few days." He set the container he had just used back down to catch more.

"Nothing to worry about, then," she said. "We'll just drown instead."

Again he laughed at her.

She hated being laughed at. He would pay for his attitude. She would see to that.

Peppe awoke at sunrise, just as he did every day he was out on the ocean. It didn't matter how much he had had to drink the night before, or how long he had worked, when the sun came up, he awoke. This second morning of his life in hell with the stupidest woman alive hadn't changed that.

She was asleep, his sweater around her shoulders as she curled against the rubber side of the dinghy. Her teeth were chattering and she was shivering. He was cold also, but from the looks of it, the day was going to be hot again. Being cold was not something that was going to hurt either of them. It was better than what they were going to be feeling by the time the heat on the ocean got done with them.

He stood on the back bench and looked around. Not a sign of land anywhere. He had hoped that the storm last night would have blown them toward an island or something, but clearly it hadn't. At the moment the wind was still pretty brisk, but that would change, he knew, by the middle of the day.

He stretched, then put his hand on his hips and

his back to the wind, then braced himself and just stood there on the bench.

"What are you doing?" she asked, waking up and looking at him.

"Stop talking," he said. "Stand up on the bench and act like a sail."

"A sail?" she asked, clearly not understanding what he was doing. "I'm happy as I am, thank you."

"Of course you are," he said, shaking his head in disgust. "You relax. I sure don't want you over-working."

"Oh, I see," she said, "you are a talking sail. In that case, Mr. Sail, could you tell me exactly which way this boat is headed?"

"I don't know," he said, giving her only part of the truth. He knew they were heading east and slightly north, but where exactly that would take them he had no idea, since he didn't know their location at the moment.

"So why are you doing such a silly game?"

"If I'm going nowhere," he said. "I want to get there fast."

He didn't add that the quicker he got away from her, the happier he would be. No point in getting her yelling at him so early in the morning.

He stood, letting the wind push against his back as he studied the horizon for any sign of land.

An hour later the wind died and he sat down, getting himself ready for another long day of baking in the sun.

By evening Amber could hardly think of anything but food. Her stomach felt like someone had a hand around it and was squeezing. Her skin was burned in a number of places and her lips chapped beyond help. It even hurt to drink, even though the hairy fisherman had forced her to a number of times.

She looked around the dinghy at the horizon. As it had been for two days, there was nothing but endless, flat sea. Not even a breeze was blowing to help them stay cool. At least with the sun going down it wouldn't be so hot.

She was using his sweater as a pillow now, staring ahead as she leaned against the rubber side of the boat. She had thought the seats on the plane were uncomfortable to sleep in. What she wouldn't give for one of those seats now.

Peppe finished doing something with his bag of supplies, then strapped it to the seat and settled down, looking like he was going to try to sleep.

"What if they don't find us tomorrow?" she asked.

He said nothing.

"I don't know if I can take another night of this," she said.

He didn't even blink or open his eyes or say anything supportive, or even snide.

"I'm ill," she said. "Really ill."

Again he said nothing.

"What will we do if we're not rescued by tomorrow?" she asked.

He opened his eyes and looked at her. "Die," he said.

Then he closed his eyes and sighed.

For the first time she actually believed him. And that scared her more than anything had ever scared her before.

12

PEPPE WAS DREAMING OF STANDING ON A DOCK, WAV-ing goodbye as the blond woman floated out to sea, screaming his name over and over. He loved the dream, because he didn't have to help her in his dream. He could just let her float away, not caring. And in his dream after she was gone, he had a party, and invited all his old girlfriends, because now he knew that none of them had really been that bad.

Suddenly the dream snapped away and she, the blond bitch American, was really yelling, jumping up and down, bouncing the dinghy like she was playing some kid's game. Only she wasn't shouting his name.

"Land!" she shouted. "Look, there's land!"

It took him a second to realize what she was say-ing, since he had spent so much time over the last few days doing his best to not listen to her.

He jumped and turned to look where she was pointing. The sun wasn't quite up yet, but there was enough early morning light to tell that a tall landmass was sticking out of the water right in their path.

He studied it, hoping against hope that it stretched in one direction or another, but after a few seconds he realized it was an island. Not a big one, but big enough to have a few good-sized hills and lots of trees and brush.

The wind was blowing them toward it, and from the best he could tell, they wouldn't miss it if he could get through the current that would try to sweep them past.

Right now he wished he had ignored her and pretended the motor had run out of gas instead of actually running it out of gas. It would be a lot easier. But she had been stupid for forcing him to keep going, and he had been stupid to do it. Now he was going to pay the price with rowing.

He bent down and got the two oars from the floor of the dinghy. He secured both in their clamps on each side of the dinghy and took his seat. With the first hard pull, he turned the raft just enough to get them headed toward the island directly, nose first.

Luckily the wind was light and the swells shallow, so they wouldn't have trouble with surf near the land. But what he was the most worried about was catching the dinghy on rocks.

"Hurry up," she said, glancing at him, then back at the island as if taking her eyes off of it might make it disappear. "I don't want the wind to change."

Peppe didn't tell her that the only thing the wind was going to do was die off as it got hotter. "Don't panic," he said instead. "We'll get there. Climb up on the nose and watch out for the reef."

"Why?" she said, moving to where he had told her to.

"Because I don't want to end up on it," he said. "Or any rocks. They will sink the dinghy."

"Crap," she said, shaking her head. "Dinghies are made for landing. They used them in all the war movies. They're virtually unsinkable."

He laughed, but she didn't hear him, or pay him any attention. Two days on a raft hadn't changed her stupidity level. Since she'd watched a few old war movies, she was an expert on dinghies now. He didn't want to ask what other movies she'd seen. More than likely if his fear about this island in front of them was true, he was going to have enough time to find out.

Over the next fifteen minutes the island grew in size in front of them, and she got more and more excited.

He just kept rowing steadily, keeping the nose of the craft pointed at the island. There was no way of telling if they were coming in at high tide or low tide. If it was low, they'd have trouble on the rocks. If it was high, he should be able to find a channel.

He had worked the raft slightly to the right side of the island, where he could see a sheltered cove and some gently sloping rocky beach. That would be the easiest place to try to land.

And for a while he actually thought they might make it all the way to shore without problems. Then, about a hundred paces from the beach, Amber said, "Rocks."

He didn't have time to turn the boat at all, even though he tried, plunging both ores into the water and pushing hard to stop their forward motion. Far too little too late. He felt the boat ground on the rocks that were just below the surface. There was a nasty tearing sound as the boat jerked to a stop, and then the sound of bubbling water.

"You hit them," she said.

He said nothing, but instead stood and moved to the front of the boat. From his best guess, the water was no more than three feet deep. And the dinghy was leaking air fast from the rips in the rubber on the right side below the waterline.

He moved around her and took the lead rope on the nose and made sure it was still securely fashioned.

"What are you doing?"

"Getting us ashore," he said.

He put on his tennis shoes, then, with the rope in his hand, he jumped off the front of the dinghy, over the rock they had caught on, to what looked like a flat-bottomed area.

His guess had been right. He went in about nipple-high before touching bottom. The water was fairly warm, and his jump startled a school of fish.

He wished he could get her to help him get the dinghy off the rocks before it was too late, but he knew that just asking her would cause more problems than it was worth.

"What are you doing *now?*" she demanded.

He made sure one more time that the rope was solidly attached to the front of the dinghy, then stepped up on the rock they had hit, made sure his footing was solid on the slick surface, and pushed backward as a swell lifted the boat.

It drifted off and away, but was clearly listing to one side. Air was bubbling out of the side and he had no doubt if he didn't get this thing on dry land shortly, he was going to lose it.

"You almost knocked me down," she said.

"Hold on and don't move," he said.

He jumped off the rock and, using all his strength, pulled the dinghy to the right, around the rocks and closer to shore.

After he had gotten it to where the water was only waist-deep on him, she jumped in, not even bothering to help him tow. She started toward the beach.

He ignored her and pulled the dinghy to the left, finding an easy path ashore. After a few long minutes of backbreaking tugging and pulling, he had the craft secured up on the sand, the rope tied around a rock. He would have to come back later and pull the dinghy farther ashore, above the high-tide mark, but for the moment it wasn't going anywhere.

Inland there were some pretty solid brush and trees above the high-water line. They covered the rocky hill. Above them a fairly tall mountain of mostly rock jutted above the trees. He stared at it for a moment, knowing that he was going to have to climb that to get a good look around.

It was already hot, even though the sun hadn't been up long. He was going to have to find water and shelter from the sun.

He turned to see what she was doing, then laughed out loud. She had gone straight ashore instead of wading around a pile of rocks and finding an easy way. Now she was stuck trying to get past some big rocks as the water splashed lightly around her. He shook his head and headed to help her.

"Wait 'til I get to a phone," she said as he got close. "I'll sue those dinghy people. Then see how many dinghies they can make."

He managed not to laugh. "It kept you afloat for a few days, didn't it?"

She looked up into his smiling face from the other side of the big rock. "I don't know what you're so happy about. I am going to sue that fuckin' company you work for, too."

He shrugged and moved around to the top of the rock that she was trying to climb to get out of the water. "Don't be in a rush. You might hurt yourself."

He leaned down, took her by the arm, and lifted her up beside him.

Suddenly having her so close made his stomach twist, not in anger or hatred, but in lust. She stared into his eyes for a long second.

Finally he broke the moment and turned and jumped down on the other side, showing her the way to smoother ground.

"I want to find a bed and a doctor," she said as she followed him up the rocky beach.

He didn't want to tell her that if his hunch was right, they were the only two people on this island. All that news would accomplish was make her mad at him. And maybe he was wrong. Maybe the island was longer than he thought, and had a fishing village of some sort. So instead he played along with her.

"What do you want a doctor for?"

"In case I have picked up some disgusting tropical diseases," she said. "Ouch!"

He turned around to see her sitting on the ground rubbing her foot.

"Be careful," he said. "The rocks are loose."

"Thank you," she said, her voice the sneering tone that only came from rich people's mouths. "I have just found that out."

"I go first to have a look around," he said. "You stay here."

She frowned up at him. "Changed your tune a bit, now we know we are on land, haven't we?"

He had no idea at all what she was talking about, so he said nothing.

"You a little bit nervous of what's going to happen once I tell my story?"

Again he managed to not laugh in her face. He indicated she should stay seated. "Just wait here."

He turned and started toward the hill.

"So you can forget about me?" she shouted at him.

"Not a chance," he muttered in Italian.

"No sir, sailor," she yelled. "I'm not letting you out of my sight. The nightmare's over for me and only beginning for you."

He just kept going as she scrambled to keep up. Any woman who was that crazy deserved to hurt herself while following her own delusions.

As he started up the rocky slope, picking his way over boulders like a monkey climbing in the zoo, she decided she could watch him just fine from the level area near the beach. She knew where he was going, and if he started down the mountain another way, she would just circle around and find him. There was no way she was going to let him escape after what he had put her through the last two days. He was going to pay, and pay dearly, as soon as she found a phone.

She moved over into some shade under a large tree that allowed her to still see the mountainside and sat, watching him climb higher and higher. The hill hadn't looked that big from the beach, but as he got smaller and smaller, she could tell it was a good twenty-five stories tall, maybe even more. She tried to remember what people looked like on the street from her fifty-second-story penthouse in the city and then compare it to how small he was looking. It had to be close to that, as best she could figure. A long ways up there.

She let her mind drift, ignoring the hunger pains. It was going to feel so great to take a long hot shower, get a good meal, climb into a comfortable bed, and sleep. She was starting to imagine exactly what she would have for breakfast that next morning, when sailor boy on the rocks above whistled for her.

The whistle made her instantly angry, breaking the great mood she was in. She was about to shout that she didn't respond to whistles when he shouted down the hill, "I'm afraid that lawsuit will have to wait."

His voice was distant and echoed, but she could still hear it just fine. She just had no idea what he had meant. Sometimes common people talked in such strange languages.

"What?" she shouted back up at him.

She wanted him to point in the direction where they would find food and a phone. From as high as he was, he should be able to see the closest village.

"They are out of lawyers!" he shouted down, his voice echoing off the rocks.

"Where there is a phone there is a lawyer!" she shouted back up at him.

"No phones, either!" he shouted back.

Her stomach twisted even more than from the hunger. She wasn't going to accept what he was saying. "Why?"

"Because we landed on a deserted island!" he shouted back. Then he started to climb back down, moving slowly.

"Deserted?" she shouted at him.

It couldn't be deserted. That wasn't possible.

He stopped and shouted back, "Nothing! No lawyers, no phones, no doctors of tropical diseases. Nothing!"

Again he started working his way back down

toward where she was. His last word echoed again around the cove and off the rocks.

She knew he couldn't be telling the truth. He must be trying to play a trick on her, giving himself time to get away before she could have him arrested. It was the only explanation.

"What are you talking about, idiot?" she shouted at him. "That's impossible. This isn't fourteen-ninety-two, for God's sake."

Clearly he didn't hear her as he just kept coming down the mountain.

She stared at him, watching him ease his way over a large rock. She decided that the only way she was going to see past his stupid game this time was go up there and have a look herself.

She stood, disgusted that she was going to have to actually do the work. Then, carefully working her way over the rocks, she started up through the brush on the same path he had taken, pushing aside branches that would scratch her or scrape her sun-burned arms.

Finally, after a few minutes of slow climbing, she was only a few hundred feet below him on the mountain. She still wasn't high enough to see anything but the cove they had landed in. The climb wasn't even winding her, even without food. Luckily she kept herself in good shape.

She kept climbing, slowly, making sure of each

step so as to not twist an ankle. She was sure that if she did that, he would just leave her.

"Why do you carry on like that?" he shouted to her. "I'm not a child. If I say it's deserted, it's deserted."

"I don't believe you," she shouted back at him. She used her hands to pull herself up and over a large rock and just kept climbing.

"It is a fact."

"Fact, my ass," she said, more to herself than him. "Where there is life there are people."

Keeping her head down and her gaze on each rock, each foothold ahead of her, she kept climbing. This idiot wasn't going to play any more jokes on her. She would see to that. All she had to do was find a phone and he would be very, very sorry for what he had put her through.

13

PEPPE WAS NOT SHOCKED THAT SHE WOULD HAVE TO climb up and see for herself. She hadn't believed anything he had told her before now, why would she believe that the island was deserted?

But still, her climbing up there made him angry. Really angry, and he wasn't sure why. He would have expected nothing else. It seemed that everything this woman did got under his skin, made his blood boil. He wished he could just walk away and never think about her again. But at the moment he was trapped with her on a small island. At least that was better than a small dinghy.

The view from the top of the hill was exactly what he had expected it to be. The island was good sized, but clearly uninhabited. He would guess that if he walked the beach, it would be a good two kilometers around. There were a number of small hills and the one big one he climbed. He had seen a small lake near the base of one hill, and a couple of streams. At least that meant they would have fresh water. Food was going to have to be up to him to do his job and catch.

The cove they had landed in looked from the peak to be the roughest on the island. On the far side was a sandy-looking beach. It also looked to be sheltered by the mountain from the prevailing winds and late-afternoon hot sun. That was where he would go. And if she didn't want to follow, fine with him.

She was now only about fifty paces below him, climbing slowly. It was clear this woman rarely, if ever, climbed anything but out of bed. She was in good shape from all the exercise on bikes that went nowhere, but she didn't know how to climb up a rocky slope. She was going to have sore hands and feet by the time she got to the top.

"There are hundreds of these little deserted islands around Greece," he said to her as she stopped to catch her breath.

"Get up there and check again," she ordered.

"No," he said flatly.

There was no reason that this woman should boss him around for one minute longer. There were just the two of them on this stupid island. Her money no longer mattered here, and the less he had to do with her, the better. He certainly didn't need to take orders from her anymore, especially when her orders were so stupid.

"No?" she asked, staring at him.

"I'm not going back up," he said. "I don't need to. I had a good look before."

"It's not your place to argue," she said.

He started to tell her that was exactly what he was going to do, but she went on talking.

"You got me lost at sea, you fucked up the engine, you can't navigate." She shook her head and started climbing again as she talked. "Oh, fuck this. I can't reason with a hairy midget."

Peppe stared at her, the anger rising in his blood like a fever. Not even his old girlfriends had been allowed to call him names like that.

"What did you call me?"

"Nothing," she said, continuing to climb toward him.

"I want to know what you said."

He was barely holding in his anger. He wanted to pick up a rock and just throw it at her. He could imagine her falling over backwards and tumbling down the hill. It would be so easy. Just one good-sized rock against the side of her head.

"Nothing," Amber said again.

"Did you just call me a midget?" Peppe demanded.

"No," she said.

"Then what did you call me?"

She stopped and looked up at him. "I called you a hairy midget."

Peppe stared at her. "You may have the grace of money, but your tongue has the grace of the gutter. Watch your mouth, Ms. Big Shot."

She seemed stunned and angry. "Are you threatening me?"

Peppe just couldn't hold his anger back any longer. "You fuckin' right I am threatening you. You listen carefully. I am fed up with you. From now on I do what I like, and I let you do what you like."

He turned and started away from her, back up the hill slightly, and sideways, going in a direction so that he would not get near her and reach the beach he had seen from the top at the same time.

"You—"

He turned back to her. "Now fuck off."

Again he turned and as fast as he dared climbed along the rock-covered slope toward the side of the island where there was the wide beach. He would have to go back to the cove and get his supplies out of the raft, but he wanted to see that beach first, and this would be the best way to get to it without having to pass and go below her.

Behind him Amber shouted, "Oh, brother, you're gonna *regret* this."

"Fuck yourself!" Peppe yelled without turning

around. His voice carried out over the ocean around them.

"Keep going!" she shouted back. "Dig a deeper grave."

"Fuck yourself, *bitch!*" he shouted again.

"Come on," she shouted. "Give me more!"

"Slut!" he shouted. Never had he called a woman that before. He was surprised the word had come out of his mouth.

"What did you call me?" she shouted.

"I called you a whore," he shouted back, still not looking around at her. "A slut!"

"You bastard," she shouted. "I'll have you shot!"

A rock clattered behind him and he turned around. She was tossing rocks at him, but with her weak throw there was no chance she could reach him.

"You got to get off this island first," he shouted at her, laughing at how stupid she looked throwing rocks at him in her fury. "Haven't you?"

"Filthy fucking deckhand!" she shouted again, throwing another rock.

"Whatever," Peppe said, shrugging and turning away.

"You're a coward, Guido!" she shouted.

"That doesn't matter to you anymore, does it, because I am out of your way now!"

"You are a mongrel dog!" she shouted at his back.

He just kept going, climbing slightly as he moved away along the side of the hill.

"You are a hybrid of something dark, disgusting, and tiny."

To himself Peppe said in Italian, "Well, let the rich bitch look after herself now that her mongrel dog has left her side."

He didn't look around again until he was certain he was around the mountain. When he did finally check to see if she was following, the rich woman was nowhere to be seen.

He laughed, and then tried to push the fact that he was actually worried about her out of his mind by repeating a few times that she just wasn't worth caring about.

Or even thinking about. Right now he had more important things to think about, such as surviving.

But he still couldn't help worrying about her.

Amber had never been so angry before. She just kept throwing rocks in his direction even after he had vanished around the ridgeline. When she found a phone she would have him tracked down and tossed in jail. He couldn't get away from her just by getting a head start. That hairy midget didn't know who he was dealing with. A few years in jail would teach him who really was in charge.

She had decided she needed to find civilization and get a meal first, and the best way was to climb a little higher to see which direction to go in. More than likely it was the same way Peppe went, but she needed to know for sure.

She eased her way upward over the rocks until she finally got to a place where she could see most of the island. The sight that greeted her twisted her stomach into a tight ball. Peppe had told her the truth. They were on an island, and from where she stood she could see three quarters of it. And nowhere was there a sign of even a small fishing village.

Panic swelled up from her stomach.

Deserted island.

And not another island in sight in any direction!

She was trapped.

Nowhere to go.

No way to call for help!

She wanted to run screaming back down the hill.

And she almost did, but at the last second she stopped and took a deep breath of the hot air.

"Control," she said aloud. "Get yourself under control."

She forced the feeling of panic and fear down into her hungry stomach. Then, using some exercise methods of breathing she had learned in the gym at home, she got her heart to slow down a little and her thoughts to clear.

Finally she was able to look around again, take stock of her situation.

The heat was starting to bake her skin and legs and feet, and it was going to get a lot warmer before it cooled down. And she was weak and very hungry. She needed to think, to figure out what to do while she still could.

She turned slowly, studying everything she could see about the island.

After a moment she found herself trying to spot Peppe. She realized what she was doing and got angry all over again. She didn't need him. Someone would come soon enough and rescue her, and then he would know the price of not following orders. She would survive just fine until then.

The anger cleared the last of the panic from her mind. She would show him.

First she needed water and food. And she wasn't going to find either on the side of this mountain. Slowly, making sure to not hurt her feet any more than they already were, she worked her way back down the hill.

By the time she reached the beach her feet were cut and bleeding and she was weak from hunger and the heat. And she had no idea what to do next.

By the time Peppe had reached the white, soft sand of the beach he had seen from the mountain, his anger at her and himself had faded. He knew she was just who she was. Money had made her the demanding, spoiled bitch.

And he had no doubt that she would fail in taking care of herself on this island. She didn't have the skills or the brains to do so. If she didn't find him by evening, he would go looking for her to make sure she wasn't hurt.

He didn't like the fact that he cared about her and felt responsible for her, but he did, and the walk down the mountain allowed him to get his anger under control.

He had no idea how she got under his skin the way she did. It was as if they were old, married people, sniping at each other's bad habits. His parents had been like that, and the only person who could make his father completely crazy with anger was Peppe's mother. They loved each other and always made up with as much passion, but growing up Peppe had not understood the anger. And he still didn't.

Now this blond bitch comes along and makes Peppe crazy angry with just one word sometimes. He was attracted to her and hated her at the same time, and there wasn't a thing he could do about it, either.

He started down the beach, checking out both the ocean gently lapping at the sand and the tree line above the high-water mark. If nothing else, he was stranded on a beautiful island. The white sand ran up into the green underbrush and trees. And the water was a deep blue, signaling perfect fishing conditions in the shallows.

He knew without even going into the water that there would be enough for him to eat in these waters.

About a hundred paces down the beach he came across a wooden fishing hut tucked just above the high-water mark. It had been built with planks on the front and roof and back, and used piled rocks on the side to give it support in the high winds. Its roof was a combination of wood and tree branches that looked as if it would leak, but still keep most of the water off anyone inside.

He tried to push open the wooden door, but it was locked with a rusted old doorknob. It popped open after a few hard shoves.

Inside it smelled of damp and mold. It was small and sparse, but yet better than what he could have built in a short time. The floor was dirt and there were no windows letting light in. He could see some light through a few slits in the roof, but it was not bad, considering.

Clearly the hut was rarely used. More than likely it had been built by someone on a nearby island as a retreat to get away and just fish and be alone.

There was an old mattress in one corner. He picked it up and banged on it to make sure nothing was living in the stuffing, then dragged it out the door and into the sun. He propped it up so that the sun and wind would dry out any mold on it.

Back inside the hut he found an old fishing net, then a Coke bottle and a brown rug torn in a few places. He took the rug outside as well and laid it over the rocks beside the hut to dry.

"This could be a lot worse," he said to himself in Italian as he studied his new home. A lot worse. Finding this would make his stay here a lot more comfortable.

He stuffed the empty Coke bottle into his belt and headed out down the beach in the direction of the cove they had landed in. He needed to find a good, clean supply of water, and then he would work on getting himself some decent food.

And maybe along the way, he would find out what was happening to good old Miss Rich Bitch. He didn't like the fact that he kept worrying about her. And he would never let her know he did. Ever.

14

AMBER FELT ANGRY, HUNGRY, AND THIRSTY. NEVER IN all her life had she been so miserable. When she got back Tony was going to pay for making her go on that stupid boat and go through all this torture.

The hour before she had managed to get off the mountain without hurting her feet too badly, but since then she was having no luck at all finding anything that looked like food or decent drinking water.

She had crossed one small stream coming down off of the hill. At first she had been glad to see it, but when she had had to jump across, she realized the water smelled bad. Or at least she thought it did, and one small pond area was filled with tiny fish swimming in it. There was no way she was going to drink out of that.

She convinced herself she wasn't *that* thirsty yet.

She followed the stream down to the ocean and

found a white sand beach that was sheltered by rocks on both sides. It wasn't more than a hundred paces long. If she was looking for a place to relax and nude sunbathe, this would be the spot. But right now relaxing seemed a long way away. She needed food and water, and with every step she could feel the need growing as she got weaker. She had had the same feelings when she exercised too hard right before dinner. Only this time it was much worse.

She walked along the water, letting the sand cool her hot and tender feet. Just where the gentle waves were breaking she found what looked like an oyster. She had eaten oysters raw before and knew she could do that, so she spent a good ten minutes trying to break open the shell. When she finally smashed it with a rock whatever had been inside was far too disgusting to ever eat. And it smelled as if it had rotted long ago.

She went back up to the tree line and sat on the sand in the shade of a large tree, staring out over the ocean. Her stomach hurt. Sometimes a dull ache, sometimes with sharp, shooting pains like bad cramps on the worst day of the month. And her lips were starting to crack from the salt and sun and lack of water. Just sitting there she felt dizzy, and she knew that wasn't a good sign.

Maybe she could follow Peppe and watch where he drank water. And if he didn't get sick, then she could drink from the same place. Clearly it was better that he test the water than she did. It would serve him right if he got sick.

She nodded to herself. She liked the idea of letting him test water for her. He would do all the work, as it should be, she would get the benefits.

She pushed herself to her feet and looked around, staring at the mountain that dominated the center of the island. The hairy Italian had stormed off toward the area to her right. And if she remembered correctly, the dinghy was to the left. She would just follow the beach around to the right until she saw him, then follow him until he tested water and food. She figured it couldn't be that far around the island.

It was a good plan.

It was a plan that would allow her to survive until help arrived and arrested him. No matter how much he shouted at her, called her names, and refused to help her anymore, he still was going to end up helping her. And that would be almost as good a revenge as seeing him in prison.

She laughed at the thought and started off down the beach, staying in the shadows, feeling the new energy from her plan.

The heat pounded the island, the sun reflecting off the smooth ocean surface, making everything seem even hotter than Peppe knew it really was.

He had worked his way along the shoreline, back to the rocky beach where they had landed, going slowly and staying under the trees as much as he could. He still hadn't gotten anything to drink or eat, and until he did he needed to be careful and conserve his energy.

The dinghy, one side completely flat, was still well secured, but he didn't feel like it would survive a big blow where it was at. And the last thing he wanted to do was come back here in a storm and try to save a half-inflated dingy.

"Do it now," he said to himself in Italian, "or forget it."

He hadn't liked the idea of forgetting it, so even though he was weak from hunger and it was almost the hottest time of the day, he pulled the dinghy another twenty paces on the beach, then tied it off to a tree. He decided that after he got some water and food, he would come back and get the dinghy all the way up into the trees and very secure. But at least now it would ride out anything but the worst storms.

He took the emergency kit, his mask, and snorkel from the dinghy, then headed back toward the shack, again staying to the shade as much as possible and moving slowly so as to not drain what energy he had left.

He dumped the supplies beside the shack, then went in the other direction down the beach to a stream he had noticed earlier. It had a pretty good flow of fresh water coming off a rock from a spring just a short distance up the hillside. That water would be as clean and fresh as any water on the island. He felt lucky to find it so close to the hut. Maybe this spring was why the hut had been built here in the first place.

He had washed out the Coke bottle a few times in the ocean on the way back from the dinghy, and he did it again a few more times now with fresh water. Then he filled it and tasted the wonderful liquid.

Clear and tasteless and cold. He had never drunk anything so perfect.

He sat in the shade and finished off two bottles, the first quickly, the second more slowly, then he refilled the bottle a third time and took it with him. On the way back to the hut he noticed a piece of rubber that had washed up on the beach and picked it up. It looked like a strap off a diving mask, or maybe part of a wet suit.

"This will work nicely," he said in Italian, studying the long shape, stretching it, then twisting it to see how much give it still had. He knew exactly what he would do with it.

He found a piece of wire sticking out of the sand near a tree a few minutes later that would help as well. He took it all and went to a shady spot a hundred paces down the beach from his cabin that had a nice, flat-topped rock he could work on like it was a table.

He used his knife to cut a strong stick from a nearby strand of brush, then he used the rubber and wire to fashion a type of speargun. It was primitive, like something a child would build, and rough in workmanship, but it would work far better than trying to catch fish with his bare hands.

He then sat back, took a sip of water, and studied the surf. Just into the waves from the flat rock was a perfect area for crab and fish. Gentle waves broke over a shallow reef twenty meters from the water line. The area between the sand and the reef should be teaming with fish yet shallow enough for him to work it without too much danger from currents.

Out there was his dinner.

The water was making him feel better, but without food he wouldn't start gaining back the strength he had lost the last two days.

He was just about done with his new weapon when he heard some noise in the brush down the beach in the opposite direction of the hut. Without letting on that he had heard anything, he watched out of the corner of his eye until Amber moved again, jumping from behind one brush to a hiding place behind a tree, acting like a child playing hide-and-seek.

She looked terrible. It had only been three or four

hours since he had left her, but now her feet looked like they were sore and bleeding. There were scratches on her arms and her face was burned. She wasn't carrying any water in anything, so Peppe had no doubt she hadn't drunk anything yet. She wasn't going to last much longer unless she did, especially in this heat.

He shook his head, half disgusted at himself. There he was again, worrying about her. But no matter how disgusting she was as a person, and spoiled by her money, he still felt responsible. He knew that was stupid. She was a grown, married woman who should be able to take care of herself, but there was just something about her that kept drawing him like a bug toward a light.

And since she was hiding from him, spying on him, she clearly knew that she needed him as well. She just didn't want to admit it. Stupid games they both played.

He finished his speargun, then took a sip of the water from the bottle so she would know what it was, and left it sitting on the flat rock as he turned and headed for the water. If she was smart, she'd come out into the open and take the water and drink it while he was fishing.

He'd better get enough fish for the both of them, from the looks of things. But if she wanted any, she was going to have to ask nicely and apologize for calling him names. He had no doubt she wouldn't like doing that, but if he was going to feed her and keep her alive, it was the least she could do.

He smiled to himself as he headed toward the water. Things were about to change between them.

As far as he was concerned, it was about time.

Amber had barely made it to where Peppe was working. She could not believe how far it was around this stupid island. It had looked so small from the mountain, but the rocks and beaches and brush had seemed to go on forever. She had cuts on her feet, and brush had scraped her arms in a bunch of places.

But the worst was her face. It felt like it might just dry up and fall off. She didn't even want to touch her lips, they were so chapped.

She had just about decided to give up and lie down under a tree for the rest of the day when she saw him. She had managed to sneak up on him as he worked on something attached to a stick.

Then, when he took a sip from a Coke bottle, she almost ran out there and grabbed it from him. She needed something to drink and she needed it badly. She was wishing now that she had drunk from the stream she had found. Even sick would be better than how she was feeling now.

Peppe set the Coke bottle down on the rock, picked up his stick, and headed for the water. She had no idea what he was doing and didn't care. All she could see was that bottle of liquid.

She made herself wait until he had waded out into the water before she darted out and grabbed the bottle.

At that moment, he turned around and looked at her.

She took a drink from the bottle, letting the best-tasting water ever wash down her throat.

He smiled at her, then put the mask in place and dove into the water.

She moved back into the trees and watched. He surfaced once, went back down again. She could see his shape through the clear water, moving about as though he belonged under there.

Then, a very short time after he went down, he came up and started toward the sand. In one hand was the biggest lobster she had ever seen, wiggling to get free. On the end of the stick was a fish, speared through and not moving.

He didn't pay her any attention at all, didn't yell at her for taking his water, so she finished off the water and openly watched as he banged the lobster on its head with a rock, then did the same to the fish.

Then, using the same knife he had used to fix the engine, he quickly cut the fish open and gutted it, leaving it on the flat rock where the Coke bottle full of water had been.

Ignoring her completely, he took a few smaller rocks and built a quick ring in the sand in the sun. Then he filled the ring with twigs and some dry grass, picked up his mask, and went back out to the surf and filled it with water.

She had no idea what he was doing, but that lobster and fish lying on the rock looked fantastic. The water she had drunk was making her stomach rumble and ache. She needed food and she needed it desperately. She could offer to buy it from him. He was poor, he wouldn't refuse that, she was sure. And besides, she would never pay him, since it was his fault she was on this stupid island. The only thing he was going to get from her was jail. But he wouldn't know that.

He used the mask full of water as a type of magnifying glass over the dried grass and sticks, holding it steady until some of the grass started smoking, then burst into flame.

He put the mask aside, slowly adding more and more sticks to the fire until it was going well. Then, using sticks balanced on rocks on either side of the fire, he put both the fish and the lobster over the heat, turning them slowly every few seconds.

The smell from the cooking fish almost made her faint. She needed to eat, and she needed to now.

He took the fish off the fire and cut a piece off of it with his knife, then filled his mouth with the wonderful-smelling meat. He sighed, chewed a few times, and then swallowed, clearly savoring the taste.

That was it. Amber had to do something *now*.

She stepped toward him, trying not to limp on her sore feet. She couldn't let him see weakness in her. She had to keep him where he belonged.

"I could have you arrested," she said.

The moment the words came out of her mouth she regretted them. That wasn't the way to get someone to give you food. She knew better than that, but her pride just couldn't let her do anything else.

He laughed and took another bite of the fish, then turned to her. "By who? The sand police? Since you have been so kind to me, you force me to give you all of my fishes."

He laughed again and took another bite. "I can see you are a very clever woman."

She could feel her face flush with anger. He was getting to her again, making her angry. She didn't know how he could do that to her.

He kept eating, not offering any to her, torturing her. He knew she was starving.

"There is a law against this," she said.

"Of course there is," he said, nodding. "I can go to prison for a thousand years for eating when hungry."

Again he laughed and she felt her anger growing even more intense.

"Is there anything else I can do for you?" he asked. "While I am waiting to get arrested."

He took another large bite of the fish. It was half gone already and she hadn't even tasted it yet. How could he do that to her? He was supposed to be working for her.

He took the lobster off the heat and carefully broke open a leg, letting the wonderful-smelling white meat drip over his hairy face as he ate it.

"I can feed myself, you know," she said. "I don't need your food."

She knew she did, but she just couldn't bring herself to ask this hairy common man who was laughing at her.

He shrugged. "Bon appetit, and bon nuit." He gathered up the lobster and the fish, picked up the mask and stick with the rubber on the end, and smiled at her. "I am going to rest."

"Sell me that fish."

"What?" he asked, staring at her with a smile on his face.

"I want what is left of that fish," she said, pointing to it. "So sell it to me."

He shook his head. "Fuck off and bother some other poor shipwrecked sailor."

She was so desperate she didn't even care that he

had just told her to fuck off. All she could see was that fish. She needed that fish. She was going to starve if she didn't get some food in her mouth soon.

"How much?"

He didn't answer as he kicked sand over the fire.

"I'll give you a hundred dollars," she said. She knew he had to have a price. Everyone had a price.

He said nothing.

"Two hundred."

He ignored her and finished kicking the sand over the fire. The fish was in his right hand, looking wonderful, better than anything she had ever been served in New York's finest restaurants.

"Okay, five hundred dollars just for the remaining half of that fish."

Peppe turned and looked at her. "If you are hungry, bake a cake."

It took her a moment to realize and understand what he had said. He must have been listening to her conversation with Todd about drugs and the blind. How dare he eavesdrop on her conversations. She was about to yell at him about that, then stopped. Food was the most important thing first.

"This is my last offer," she said. "One thousand dollars. And my gold bracelet. Take it, okay. Now give me some fish!"

He shook his head and turned to walk away.

She couldn't believe it. He wasn't going to sell her the fish, even for a thousand dollars. He really was crazy.

He turned and looked at her. "I am not interested. This fishes is not for sale. There are a thousand more fishes where this came from, but this one fishes is not for sale."

She shook her head, not understanding what he was saying.

"There are some things in life that can't be bought, and this fishes is one of them."

She was so angry and so sick she didn't know what to do. He was holding her up for ransom. He couldn't do that, but he was.

"But I am hurt and I need a good meal," she said, stepping toward him. "Ten thousand fuckin' dollars for the half fish."

"Let me quote the laws of capitalism," he said. "The proprietor of goods can set any price he or she sees fit and shall not be at the mercy of ethical or moral issues."

"Give me some of that fish, scumbag!"

She reached for the fish in his hand and he slapped her, hard, directly across her face.

The slap stopped her cold in her tracks and she just stared at him.

No one had ever treated her like that.

No one had ever slapped her like that before, either.

No one.

The stinging on the side of her face seemed to radiate down her body.

He had slapped her.

Yet she couldn't move, couldn't shout back, couldn't do a thing but stand there and stare at him.

15

PEPPE COULD NOT REALLY BELIEVE HER ATTITUDE. SHE was starving, hurting from cuts and scratches, and being baked alive by the sun. Yet she still wouldn't do anything to get some of his food but threaten him or offer to buy it.

She had taken his water, then when he had told her his food wasn't for sale, she had tried to grab it from him. It was true, the rumor that the rich have no morals. Just to stop her he had slapped her.

In all his life he had never imagined slapping a woman who had so much money. He had slapped many women over the years, but always when they got out of line. Or when they slapped him first. And even if they were poor, he had often regretted doing it the moment the slap happened.

But now it felt like it was far, far overdue. If ever there was a woman who needed to be slapped, it was this one, as far as he was concerned.

She just stood there, staring wide-eyed at him.

He said nothing. He hadn't even hit her hard enough for his hand to sting, but clearly she had never been slapped before. He expected her to come at him like a tiger protecting her cubs, but this woman was full of all sorts of surprises.

And so was he.

She just stood there, her eyes out of focus, as if she had actually enjoyed him slapping her. He had heard of women like that.

But even if she had enjoyed it, he decided right at that moment that if she needed his food, then just like any normal person, she would have to pay for the food, and not with her husband's dirty money. She would have to earn it herself.

He stepped closer to her and she flinched, as if afraid he was going to slap her again. Good. She needed to be afraid of him. He wanted her to learn some respect.

"New rule number one," he said, his voice low and cold and level, "don't ever insult me again."

She didn't move.

"Number two, I am the boss now."

She blinked on that, but again said nothing.

"Number three, if you want food from me, you are going to have to earn it. I do not care for your husband's money."

Again she blinked and said nothing.

"To earn this food, you must wash my clothes."

He had started to take off his pants when she finally got her voice back.

"You can't hit a woman, you fuckin' lunatic."

He slapped her again, right across the cheek.

This time the blow stung his hand and turned her head. The sound echoed over the beach and died off.

"Don't forget the number one rule," he said. He took off his pants and tossed them at her.

"From now on fishes is the plural for fishes," he said.

She looked puzzled for a moment, then nodded.

He went on. "If you are back within one hour with my clothes cleaned and sundried and folded, I shall consider fishes for you."

"Can I at least have something to eat first," she said, her voice a soft whine.

He laughed, remembering her conversation back on the boat with Todd. "Did you give your drugs to the needy before they paid for them?"

She said nothing.

"Well, we don't accept credit in this house, either. And number four rule, call me Mr. Esposito."

"What?"

"No," he said, shaking his head. "I like *master*. Call me master."

"Master?" she asked, clearly not believing what he was forcing her to do.

Peppe shook his head in disgust. There was no amount of slapping that was going to change anything about this woman. She was beyond help.

"Go!" he shouted at her. "Go! Leave me! Go find your own food."

A look of panic overwhelmed her face and she stepped toward him. "Where the fuck am I going to find a washing machine on a deserted island?"

He stared at her, letting his anger show.

"Master," she said, as an afterthought.

"That is not my problem," he said.

He slipped his fingers into the band on his underwear and slipped them off, standing in front of her completely naked. She glanced at his crotch, then stared at it.

He looked down at his own manhood, then back at her. "Frightened?"

She took a deep breath and stared him right in the eye. "Mr. Esposito, this is unfair. You are completely taking advantage of me."

He laughed. "Of course I am. I am the master."

He had slapped her twice. And then exposed himself. He was going to die for that once Tony discovered what he had done.

And even after slapping her the hairy Italian wouldn't give her any food, even though he was supposed to be taking care of her, working for her. She had heard that mutiny was punishable by death, and she was going to be glad to see him dead, that was for sure.

The two slaps had startled her in another way. Never had she had a forceful man order her around. Tony would never think of hitting her, and she controlled him as if he were a puppet. She had to admit that Tony's passiveness sometimes disgusted her. She had always wondered what it would be like to be with a strong, controlling man. She just didn't expect to run into one who was a peasant.

She had decided when he took his clothes off that it was now best to just humor the man. There was no telling what kind of acts he was capable of. She had to admit, he was a finely muscled, well-endowed man. In fact, never had she seen a man so well hung, and the way he stood there, naked in front of her, told her that he knew it.

If she didn't hate him so much, she might actually be interested in a little fling.

She had taken his clothes and started off down the beach toward a stream. She figured that if she washed out his clothes in the stream and then spread them over rocks in the hot sun, they'd be dry in an hour. And she could get some food.

She found the stream and while bending over dipping his clothes in the water, the dizziness from the lack of food caught up with her and she went forward onto her hands and knees in the cold water.

"Fuckin' peasant," she said, sitting back and taking deep breaths so that the spinning would stop. "I'll have him electrocuted."

The thought of him dying for his crimes against her kept her going. That, and the image of that wonderful fish.

Her stomach hurt worse as she lay in the shade, waiting for his clothes to dry. The water she had drunk had helped, but not much. She knew she needed food and she needed it soon.

She must have dozed a little because when she awoke, the entire beach was in the shadows and the sun was low on the horizon.

She moved too quickly and everything spun, as if she were on a merry-go-round spinning way too fast.

After a few deep breaths, she managed to get to her feet. It took a moment for the dizziness to pass completely before she could move to get his clothes off the rocks. It took a few minutes more to fold them into something that looked neat.

Somehow she made it back down the beach to where the fish and half-eaten lobster still sat on the rock. He had started another fire, a better one this time, and was sitting naked waiting for her.

She handed him the pile of clothes and then turned to get some fish.

"I want you to say, 'Thank you, Master, for the privilege of washing your clothes.'"

She stopped and turned to him, wanting to call him every name in the book. He just sat there smiling, looking at her. With the food so close, she didn't dare call him anything but what he asked. She had to play his stupid games.

She took a deep breath and said, "Thank you, Master, for letting me wash your clothes."

Each word hurt, as if she were spitting out sand. Never in all her life had she allowed herself to be so humiliated. Or so controlled by anyone.

She again turned for the food.

"Where do you think you are going?" he demanded.

She stopped.

He stood and moved to a place in front of her, just standing there. She forced herself to keep her gaze locked on his eyes.

"Enough, Peppe," she said, swaying. "I need to eat."

He slapped her, firmly across the same cheek he had slapped before.

She staggered sideways, the stinging in her cheek as if she had put her face on a hot burner. Her head was aching and she was getting dizzier by the moment.

"Have you learned nothing?" he shouted at her.

She fought to listen, to stay on her feet, as he talked.

"Who is Peppe? Get in line, woman!"

He handed her the empty Coke bottle and pointed to the rock where water was flowing. "I want this bottle filled with water, and be quick about it."

She desperately wanted to shout at him, claw his eyes out, but she needed the fish. She needed food and a good night's sleep.

And she needed him to stop slapping her.

She couldn't stand any more slaps.

She nodded and took the bottle. Staggering and limping, moving as carefully as she could to protect her sore feet, she headed toward the rock with the water flowing over it.

"What?" he asked behind her.

"Yes, Master," she said, loud enough for him to hear.

She would have him killed when this was over.

She took a long drink of water at the rock, filled the bottle, drank all of it, then refilled it again and brought the bottle back to him. He had dressed in his freshly washed clothes and was sitting in the sand watching the sun set over the smooth ocean.

She handed him the bottle and he nodded to the food.

In all her life she had never tasted fish so good, or lobster so perfect. It was everything she could do to force herself to slow down and chew everything. Since she hadn't had food in her stomach in two days, she needed to not eat too much. She knew that from reading a book about fasting.

But it tasted so good, it was hard to go slow. Impossible.

Peppe sat, drinking his water, watching her ravish her food as the sun set. She didn't even have enough common sense and self control to eat slowly. He started to warn her, then shrugged. If she wanted to make herself sick that was her problem, not his.

After a moment he couldn't stand watching her anymore. He stood and headed back toward the hut.

"Where are you going?" she asked between mouthfuls.

He ignored her and just kept going.

"What about an answer?" she demanded. "It's rude not to answer."

He just shook his head in disgust. Nothing was going to teach this woman manners. Her husband's money had spoiled her beyond all hope.

"Wait for me," she shouted at him.

He just kept walking.

"Please!" she said, her voice now with a touch of panic. "Wait. I've hurt my foot."

Peppe paid her no attention. He got to the hut and checked to see if the mattress had dried. It had. He banged it a few times to clear out the dust and anything that might be hiding in it, then opened the door to put the mattress inside.

"My God!" Amber said, limping up in front of the

hut, part of the lobster in one hand. "Where did this come from? Thank goodness, a roof!"

He moved the mattress inside and put it in the corner. Clearly she was thinking that she was going to sleep inside with him. The last thing he wanted was that to happen. He could barely stand her as it was. He had found this hut and he was going to sleep in it. And she wasn't.

"A bed!" she shouted, clapping her hands together. "I am saved."

He stepped inside and slammed the door in her face as she started inside.

There was a moment of silence, then she said, "What are you doing, Mr. Esposito? I mean, *Master.*"

He said nothing to her as he straightened up the bed and put his jacket on it as a small blanket.

"You can't leave me out here. It's cold out here."

He almost laughed out loud at that. It was going to get cold before the night was past, but at the moment the day's heat still kept the air very warm.

"I can't survive another night outside," she said. "I am not an animal."

He would have been able to make a good argument with that statement, but he didn't. There was no point since the woman never listened to anything but her own selfish thoughts.

She banged on the door, rattling the entire hut.

He opened it. "What do you want?"

She said nothing.

"Oh, you want to share my bed?"

She looked shocked, but again said nothing.

"What kind of person are you? You wish to corrupt me? I am the master and you are the slave."

He stepped back and slammed the door in her face again. He could hear the sound echo over the still ocean and off the rocks above.

"Don't flatter yourself," she said, loud enough for him to hear.

"Pigs keep warm with leaves," he said, insulting her but at the same time giving her the way to keep warm when it got cold. Even in his insults he was trying to take care of her.

"Pigs?" she asked, her voice now angry. Clearly the fish had given her strength back, at least enough to return to the bitch she always was.

"I would fuck a pig, then kiss you, monkey boy."

He opened the door, stepped toward her, and slapped her again. The blow twisted her head around and she almost went down.

"You forgot yourself again, woman," he said. "Let the chill of the night try to wrestle the last of the beast from within you."

He stepped back into the hut and shut the door.

Then he latched it so she couldn't get in while he was sleeping. He stretched out on the mattress and let out a deep sigh. It felt wonderful.

Outside he could hear her whimpering, muttering to herself, moving around a little, but he paid her no attention. She would survive the night if she didn't do anything really stupid.

And if she did something stupid and got killed, then so much the better for the world, as far as he was concerned.

16

AMBER HAD JUST MADE IT THROUGH THE WORST NIGHT
of her entire life. She had thought the nights on the
dinghy were bad, but nothing like this first night on
the island.

That damned hairy Italian hadn't let her into the
hut, or use the bed. He had hit her four times, and
she still didn't know what to do about it.

Clearly he had been playing some control game,
and considering how hungry she had been, she had
had no choice but to play along.

Right after dark her stomach had rebelled, and she
had lost the fish and lobster she had eaten. She vaguely
remembered lying in the sand under some trees, throwing up and being too weak and dizzy to even move.

Finally, at some point, she had managed to stagger
down the beach in the starlight to the rock with the
water and clean out her mouth, wash off her face,

and drink a little. By then the night air was starting to get cold, and she had no protection.

She ended up curled in a ball, sleeping fitfully, against the door of the hut, dreaming about a full table of food that no one would allow her to get near.

She awoke just as the sun was starting to light up the ocean when he opened the door, causing her to fall inside the hut to the dirt floor.

She sat up quickly, but then decided she better not stand yet, as the room spun as if she had been drinking for days. Her stomach was rumbling and she was shivering from the cold.

"I want my room cleaned and my clothes ready by the time I return," he said, standing over her.

She staggered to her feet, holding on to the side of the door as he yawned and then started to take off his clothes again. He tossed his pants at her feet. "Remember, by the time I return."

"But—" She started to complain, then something inside her just snapped back to her old strength. "Jesus Christ! Isn't this game over yet?"

He stepped forward and, before she could even raise an arm, he slapped her again, so hard that she banged her head into the door.

"Next rule," he said, staring at her as if he might hit her again. "No blasphemy. You have a mouth like a sewer. Clean it out, and clean this room. No work, no food."

He walked out and she stood there, letting the stinging in her cheek fade. There was going to be no end to this game, she could see it now. Until someone rescued her and arrested him, she would have to play along if she wanted to survive.

She didn't like to admit also that there was something very alluring about him, and his control of her. That wasn't the way she had been taught to think. She controlled everything, even her husband, and she had made sure that everyone around her knew it. Suddenly a peasant from Italy, a simple fisherman, had broken her control, and was turning her into his own slave. That angered her, disgusted her, and attracted her at the same time. Conflicting thoughts that she was sure would clear away the moment she was rescued and got a good night's sleep and a few meals.

Until then she would have to play his games, and there didn't seem to be anything she could do about it. Tony, her money, her family could not help her here.

She pushed herself away from the door of the hut where she had been leaning and went to work cleaning up the hut, brushing out old twigs and leaves, making sure the old mattress was smooth. She then folded his clothes and put them neatly on the bed for his return.

She desperately wanted to lie down on the mattress and sleep, but she had no doubt that if he found her like that when he got back, he would hurt her a lot more than slapping her. And worse yet, he might turn her away and not give her any food.

To survive this, she needed food. And to get food, she needed to play his game.

He got back ten minutes later, looked around the hut, and nodded. Then he turned to her. "We go find fishes for breakfast."

He picked up his stick with the rubber attached and the snorkel and mask and started toward the ocean.

She said nothing, just followed him down to the waves like the slave he was making her into.

"Stand in the water there," he said, pointing to a spot out about ten feet. "When I give you fishes, you take them and put them on the sand here." He dug a dip into the sand a few feet above the waves.

She nodded.

He went into the water and she followed to the spot he had indicated, the warm water lapping at her knees. Standing in the ocean felt good and cleared her head some. But it also made her realize just how hungry she really was.

He kept going, wading out another ten steps to a spot waist-deep. She watched as he put on the mask and dove forward.

She could see him down through the clear blue water, and almost before she realized what had happened, he was back up with a large flat fish on the end of the spear.

He stepped toward her, extended the spear and fish.

She got both hands around the slimy thing and tried to pull it free, but it wiggled and she lost her grip.

"Quick, woman," he said. "You are not fast enough. The fishes are getting away."

"I am trying, Master," she said, almost choking on the word *master*. "I am trying."

She yanked the fish off the spear with both hands, then, being careful to not drop it, she turned and headed for the sand.

"Trying is not good enough," he said. "You have to work harder."

He turned and dove back under the water.

"I'm not a fuckin' donkey," she said to herself as she dropped the fish into the hole in the sand and turned to go back to her spot, washing her hands off in the gentle waves as she did.

But a little voice in the back of her head said, *Oh, yes, you are a donkey, and you deserve it.*

A moment later Peppe surfaced and she had to move quickly to yank a second fish off his spear before he got angry at her.

It took him less than twenty minutes to spear ten fish. That would be enough for both of them for the day. Amber had actually been a good help after he got her trained and she sped up.

He had her help him carry the fish from the beach back up to the flat rock, where he sorted them into what they would have for breakfast, lunch, and part of dinner.

He got the fire started again and had Amber tending it, letting it grow just enough to cook the fish. He had found in one corner of the hut a metal fire rack, so while she kept the flames going, she carried some rocks into position to hold the cooking rack. It would allow the fishes to cook more uniformly than on sticks.

"Master," she said.

Peppe didn't even bother to look at her, but he was glad she was at least under enough control now to use the word *master*. He didn't really want to be her master, but it was the only way he could think of to control her.

"What?"

"If you are decent to me," she said, her voice low and soft, "I will see that you are rewarded."

Peppe stopped sorting the fish and turned to stare at her. There was no doubt one of her stupid rich person's games. "Money?" he asked.

"Yes, if you would like," she said.

"Why do you insult me? You offer money that you didn't even work for."

She started to object but he went on. "At least a whore works for her bread."

She looked shocked.

"You know how to gut fishes?" he asked. "You know how to scale one?"

"Do I look like I would?" she said.

He let her get by without saying *master* that time. "I will show you once. After that, it is your job."

He could tell she didn't like the sound of that.

"And from now on you cook, you clean, and you prepare everything."

She was staring at him, and he could tell she wasn't liking the idea at all. And why would she? She had been a rich woman who had had people like him waiting on her every whim. Now she was the poor one and had to do the work and she wasn't liking it at all.

"Is that clear?" he asked, staring at her.

"Yes."

This time he wasn't going to let her get away without the right phrase.

"What?" he asked.

She swallowed, then said, "Yes, Master."

He nodded. "How do you know they will come?" he asked.

She looked startled at the question but said nothing.

"How do you know anyone will come and rescue us? How do you know that we won't have to spend years on this island?"

She looked totally shocked. He could tell she

hadn't thought about that at all. That was typical of her. He doubted she had ever thought about anything beyond the evening's meal before.

"I'll kill myself," she said.

He laughed and waved his arm at the trees and mountain over them. "Go ahead. But as long as you breathe, you work. Now get to the fish."

She slowly stood, dropping her stick into the fire and stepping toward the rock. She was moving slowly, clearly fighting him. And he couldn't allow that.

As she passed he kicked her in the ass, just hard enough to cause her to stumble forward before catching her balance.

She spun on him. "Why do you keep assaulting me?"

He ignored her question. "The party is over," he said. "You wait on me now."

He spun her by the shoulder and kicked her in the ass harder this time. Then he pointed at the fish. "Move!"

"You're hurting me," she said, stumbling through the sand to where the fish lay on the flat rock.

"I will show you how to clean fish," he said, angry that she had complained again. He would show her that there would be no complaining. "First you must kiss the master's hand."

"Pardon?" she said, staring at him.

"Kiss it!" he ordered, holding out his hand. "You

will be punished every time you disobey me, just like you used to do to me."

Her face paled at that, but she didn't kiss his hand.

"You made me spit blood," he said, "waiting on your every need. Even yesterday you still called me disgusting names. So now kiss the master's hand."

She didn't move.

"Kiss it!"

Tears slowly formed in her eyes, running down her sunburned cheeks.

He knew he had to keep pushing. "You can kiss my hand, follow my orders, or you can leave. It is *your* decision."

She stared at him, tears flowing down her face.

"But if you leave," he said, "you leave forever. Understand? You can leave and accept the terms of nature, or stay and accept my terms."

He thrust his hand forward. "Kiss!"

She started to move to kiss his hand and he grabbed the back of her head, holding a big handful of her hair, and forced her head down to his hand.

He could feel her dry lips on the back of his hand, combining with her tears.

17

It took Amber only a few minutes to walk to the water rock, refill the Coke bottle, take a long drink herself, refill it again, and then return. The morning had grown hot, and now the full force of the heat had returned. She had a memory of being cold last night, but the heat of the day had long ago erased the feelings of it.

Both of her feet had cuts on them that looked like they were infected. And she kept getting dirt and sand in the cuts, but at the moment there wasn't anything she could do to protect them.

Peppe had mentioned that they should go to the dinghy later in the day to get it pulled up into the trees and secured, and then bring back anything they might be able to use. She wasn't sure she could walk that far, but she had no doubt he was going to force her to.

But first, he had said, they needed to have a big lunch, to get their strength up. Earlier that morning he had showed Amber how to gut and scale fish. As far as she was concerned, it was a disgusting task, but she had no choice. If she was going to eat, she had to work for him, do what he told her to do, and that was one job he was forcing on her.

He also showed her how to cook fish over the fire, and she had put the fish on to cook before she went for the water. When she got back it looked as if he was napping, his eyes closed, his face relaxed. When he was that way she had to admit he was actually very handsome.

The smell from the cooking fish was wonderful, and made her stomach twist. She would eat this meal even slower than she had the half fish he had given her for breakfast. No way did she want to get sick again. Last night had been enough of a nightmare.

She put the water on the flat rock and sat down in the sand, easing the pain on her sore feet.

Peppe opened one eye and looked at her. "Why are you sitting down?"

"Why not?" she asked. "I've worked, I've earned it."

"Get up!" he shouted at her, now fully awake and looking like he might stand and strike her at any moment. "I want to be waited on."

Amber could not believe what she was hearing.

Who did this stupid fisherman think he was, anyway? She struggled to her feet and moved to the fire to get a fish for him.

"Did you invite me to your table on the boat?" he asked. "Now it's time for you to serve me. You will eat after I am finished."

She took one fish off the fire, put it on a large leaf, and handed it to Peppe.

He took the fish and looked at her. "Remember the abuse I took from you?"

She didn't, but she didn't say anything.

"This grapefruit is too warm," he said, mimicking a woman's voice, "the fish is bad, the coffee's too old."

She couldn't believe what he was saying. He had been paid to wait on them. Tony paying for a crew to wait on them was the point of the trip. So why was he now complaining about doing what he had gotten paid to do?

"Remember sweaty T-shirts?" he asked. "Remember that game you played?"

She said nothing.

"So go on, impress me," he said, waving one arm at the trees behind them. "Give me grapefruit juice."

"Master, please," she said, falling to her knees in front of him. She could play the game as well as he could. She would play her role if she had to, for as long as she had to. Then he would pay for doing this to her.

"Go on," he said, waving her away. "Grapefruit juice. Find me some."

He reached out with one foot and shoved her away. She twisted around and ended up sprawling facedown in the sand.

"This is a nightmare," she said to herself. The worst nightmare she had ever had, and from this one she couldn't figure out a way to wake up.

She turned to climb to her feet. He was eating his fish and staring at her butt.

She looked away from him, now very worried. If this game went any farther, she might not have a choice but to try to survive without him. There was no way in hell she would ever sleep with him. The thought was too disgusting for words. But there was a good chance that if he got any crazier, he might try to rape her. That she would have to stay on guard for.

He noticed that she was glancing at him and sat back, putting his feet up on a rock. "Dance for me."

"What?" she asked, standing and staring at him.

"I said dance for me." Again his voice had that edge of anger in it. She had to stop questioning him if she was going to keep from being hit again.

But with this demand she couldn't stop herself. "There is no music."

"Make some then," he said, waving away her protest while taking a bite of the fish. "Sing as well."

"But I don't know how," she said. The last time

she had sung anything was back in school, and that was only a school song.

He leaned forward, staring at her. "You are making me angry."

She stared at him. This idiot was going to make her dance and sing for him, and there wasn't a thing she could do about it. Now she had another reason to have this hairy Italian executed when they got off this island.

She started moving back and forth, shifting her weight from one foot to another, dancing like she used to dance with boys on slow dances.

"Sing!" he ordered.

She started to murmur a song she remembered from a play she had seen some time back. She couldn't remember the name of the song, or even a large part of the words, but she would have to make do.

"Sing, I said!" he bellowed at her, his voice echoing over the water. "I don't want the sound of dirty cats in alleys, I want singing."

She forced her voice to get louder, the sound harsh and wrong even to her ears.

His eyes got a dazed, faraway look, as if he were watching something that was not there. Then finally he shook his head and said, "Enough."

He sat back, staring out over the water, ignoring her, clearly thinking whatever perverted thoughts he normally thought.

She quickly took one fish from the fire and moved to the far side of the flat rock and sat down, her back to him. Maybe if he couldn't see her, he wouldn't notice her.

Maybe that was the same way he had felt about her on the ship?

She shook the thought away. No, he was getting paid for his work on the ship. She was a prisoner here. That was different.

She took a bite of the fresh, tender fish, letting the light flavor melt in her mouth and calm her rumbling stomach.

After lunch they went down the beach to a large stream flowing off the mountain and into the ocean. "Wash the dishes here," he said, indicating a spot with a bank he could sit on just above the water. The dishes he was talking about was the fireplace grill, the Coke bottle, and the other few items he had scrounged for cooking, including a pot left behind in the hut. They needed to be washed every day, and she might as well get into the habit of doing it, as far as he was concerned.

He sat down on the bank to watch her work as she stepped gingerly in to the cold water of the large stream and began to wash the fire grill.

From his position, and how she was bending over, he had a perfect view of her fine ass. Even though she was a disgusting woman, she had a fine body, fit for a king. She was strong, in good shape, and well proportioned. He had seen almost all of her body on the ship when she and her friend sunbathed. If she wasn't so much of a bitch, she would have made someone a wonderful wife. Maybe her husband, Tony, put up with her now just because of her body. Peppe had known men who had put up with a lot more from women for a lot less of a return.

In fact, he wasn't sure why he was putting up with her at the moment.

She looked back at him.

Her questioning look made him angry. Why couldn't this woman get it through her head that she was doing his bidding now, that he was the boss, and that she couldn't question his every action?

"I can stare at you as much as I want, woman," he said. "You think I am staring at your ass? Big deal." He spit into the sand beside him and then took another swig of water from the Coke bottle.

She stood there, defiantly listening, the shallow water swirling around her legs.

"As if I would stare," he said, going on. "Besides, what about when you and your friends were sprawled out in the sun with your tits hanging out?"

She looked stunned at his question.

"Yes, tits," he said. "You showed us your tits

and most of your bodies as if we didn't exist. Remember?"

She looked like he had gotten through to her. She almost blushed, then turned back to finish washing the dishes.

"Of course you remember," he said. "Dirty slut!"

He waited for her to react as she had done the last time he called her that. All she did was stiffen her back and keep washing.

"Show me your tits," he said, deciding to see just how far he could push this woman. "Come on, uncover them."

She ignored him, staying bent over with her ass toward him, washing the pans.

He scooted forward and nudged her on her ass with his foot. "Hear me?" he asked as she stepped slightly away from him. "Are you bashful?"

He laughed, long and hard. "Madam's bashful. How come you were not embarrassed before?"

Again she didn't answer his question. He stood and kicked her hard, shoving her forward more into the running water. "You are all sprawled out in the sun on the yacht, and us dying of lust."

She caught her balance before she sprawled into the water.

"I said undress!"

She whirled around and faced him. "You filthy pig!" she shouted, her face red with anger.

He laughed.

She threw the pot at him.

He ducked just in time to catch only a glancing blow on the side of the head.

He stepped toward her and kicked out again, pushing her so hard backwards that she fell into the water. He rubbed the side of his head as she stood, completely soaked.

"Ahh," he said, "so now you're fighting back at last."

He waded into the water and grabbed her.

"Let go of me," she shouted, trying to yank away.

"I'll teach you a lesson," he said, his anger barely under control.

She fought to get away, pulling back from him. The cold river water splashed both of them, chilling his skin and sharpening his senses.

"Help!" she shouted, then twisted out of his grasp, moving backward to get away.

He followed her, staying right with her step for step.

"Help!" she shouted, her call echoing off the mountain and disappearing out over the calm, blue water of the ocean. Even the water in the stream seemed to be ignoring her.

"Go on," Peppe said, laughing as followed her step by step into the center of the wide stream. "Shout!"

"Help!" Then she screamed, now clearly panicked at what she thought he was going to do to her.

Again he had her afraid of him, and that was exactly the way he wanted her.

He lunged out and grabbed her. She wrestled with him, finally yanking free as he slipped on a rock in the river.

She turned and headed for the bank, splashing water ahead of her.

He followed, moving quicker and with less splashing.

She moved up the sandy beach with him less than two steps behind. He reached out and grabbed her and she screamed.

They tumbled into the sand. For a moment he thought he really had gotten hold of a real live tiger. She twisted and turned and kicked and fought, but he managed to stay ahead of her until she grabbed a handful of his hair and yanked his head down, causing him to let go of his grip on her.

She scrambled to her feet, he did the same, but then she turned and kicked him hard, right between his legs.

The pain shot up through his body as he doubled over, working to keep his breath and his feet.

She stepped up and hit him right in the side of the head with her fist, knocking him over.

As he fell, she kicked him again.

He had been in a lot of fights in his day. He had to admit, this woman was tough when she wanted to be. But she didn't know who she was dealing with.

As she went to kick him again while he was done, he reached out and grabbed her leg and yanked, sending her sprawling to the sand on her back.

He was up and over her instantly, trying to hold her down as she struggled.

"Run, you little vixen," he said,

She forced him to roll over with her once, but he ended back on top.

"You coward," she said, right into his face. "Rapist! Scum! Shit!"

He laughed.

"You let go of me, you pig!"

She managed to twist one arm free and punched him hard, then she tried to scramble away on her hands and knees.

He followed her, ignoring the pain from her punch and the continuing pain in his crotch from her kick. He hadn't hit her yet, and he didn't plan on doing so.

"Why should I pay for all of life's injustices?" she demanded, kicking sand at him as he got closer again. "You are obsessed."

"Obsessed with justice," he said. "I agree."

"Get away from me, you maniac!"

He grabbed her again, but didn't get both arms in his hold. She hit him again square in the nose and he could feel it starting to bleed.

"Too easy, my dear," he said. He twisted her to the sand and sat on her, holding down her arms so she couldn't throw any more punches, or reach him with any kicks. She was a strong one, but only strong from exercise. He was strong from work and fighting all his life.

"What are you doing?" she demanded, struggling to get free. Then she started screaming.

"I'm going to finish this off," he said.

She screamed again, but he ignored her and went on answering her question.

"I am going to destroy you," he said. "And make you feel what a real man is like."

She screamed again, fighting even harder to get away after he told her that. But he had her down and she wasn't going anywhere fast.

"You've never known a real man," he said.

The look of complete panic on her face was what he wanted to see.

He moved to kiss her, but she avoided him, moving her face from side to side. He pinned her head to one spot and then put a good, long kiss on her chapped lips.

At first she struggled, then slowly he could feel her soften, her muscles moving to hold him instead of push him away.

He kept the kiss going, putting his passion for her into it, until he could feel her passion respond as she held him now, moving into the kiss like a hungry animal needing food.

Finally, he broke off the kiss and pulled back so he could see her face. It was flushed, her eyes slitted. He knew that she wanted him the same way he wanted her.

"I hate you," he said to her, staring into her eyes. She was no longer struggling in any fashion. "But I also like you, and you know it."

She said nothing, so he went on. "I liked you on board the yacht, too."

She pushed up into him, not in an effort to escape, but in a movement of passion under him.

"Come on, say it," he said. "Confess your burning desire."

She moaned and again pushed up into him.

"Come on, say it," he said. "Do you have the courage to say what you are feeling inside?"

He stopped undoing his shirt, teasing her with the openness of his chest.

She moaned once more, pushing at him, but saying nothing.

"You're bursting with desire," he said. "I hear how you moan, how you feel under me. Confess your desire. Come on, say it. Admit it. You want it. Your body is saying yes, you slut."

She was breathing hard, her eyes closed. She nodded, slowly, then said, "Yes, Master. Yes."

Peppe stopped and got off of her. He knew that was what he could get her to do, but that wasn't what he wanted her to do.

"Well, it's a *no!*" he shouted at her. "Because I am saying no."

She sat up and looked at him, clearly stunned.

Then she tried to slap him, but he pinned her down again. Then he stood and yanked her to her feet, yanking her arm behind her back with one hand while grabbing a handful of her hair with another.

Then into her ear he said, "You must fall in love."

She struggled, but he held her tight.

"Head over heels in love. You are already my slave. I want you as a love slave. You'll crawl at my feet and beg for mercy, your loins will burn with desire and crazy passion, like a sickness."

Now she had gone slack in his grasp, as if his words had taken all the energy from her.

"I'll get under your skin, into your head, into your heart. Is that clear? It will be either passion or nothing."

He shoved her roughly to the sand, then turned and walked away.

"You don't know yet who Giuseppe Esposito is," he said.

Behind him he heard her break into tears.

He didn't even bother to look back.

18

AMBER HAD NEVER FELT SO TORN APART EMOTIONALLY or physically before. Nor had she ever been so confused. She had been deathly afraid that Peppe would rape her. He had been headed in that direction, it seemed, with all his looks and stares and controlling actions.

She had fought him hard when it started, hitting him, kicking him, everything, but not once had he hit her back. And then when his kiss changed her mind about wanting him, melted her resistance as if it were butter in a warming dish, he had said no.

He, a common Italian, had said no to her when she wanted him. At first that had made her angry, but with his every movement the rest of the day yesterday, the anger she was feeling had gone away, replaced with the strongest feelings of lust she had ever experienced.

He had forced her to sleep outside again last night and she hadn't even minded. She had taken some branches and used them for a slight cover as she slept on the sand. It hadn't been comfortable, but for the moment that didn't seem to matter anymore.

She had helped him fish this morning, cleaned and cooked the fish, and then cleaned up the dishes. And she hadn't minded doing that, either.

About four hours after the sun came up he announced he was going to go hunting and that she was free to do what she wanted until he got back.

She had gone and taken a bath in the river, washed out her cuts the best she could, and her clothes, and then had lain in the sun for the hour it took for everything to dry.

Now she was back near the hut, sitting on a slight hill in the shade of the trees. Suddenly to her left she heard a sound.

Peppe shouted, "Yes!"

She moved quickly down to the beach over the rocks.

"You want to eat?" he asked, holding up what looked like an octopus. "Or do you want to starve? There are no supermarkets here."

He tossed the slimy thing to her—she caught it but the feel of the wiggling suckers was too much and she dropped it.

He shook his head. "I'll get it again."

She tried to find it, but it was gone, vanished into the water.

"Firewood," he said to her.

She nodded and got up at once, moving to where she had seen some good wood. A few minutes later she was back in camp with as much as she could carry in her arms.

Peppe had recaptured the octupus and, as she watched, he skewered it with a stick. Then he suspended the octopus over the fire and looked up at her.

She held his gaze for a long time, and he did not turn away. She was close to tears.

And she wanted him more than she could ever imagine wanting a man before now.

"You are cruel," she said softly.

He said nothing.

She fought back the tears, not really understanding what she was doing. She knew she had to be with him. She knew now she couldn't survive without him.

She moved toward Peppe, looking him in the eye, seeing him through the blurred vision of tears. When she reached him, she dropped to her knees, bent over, and kissed his feet.

He said nothing.

She stroked his legs, moved her kisses upward, stroking his calves, kissing his knees.

Desire for him boiled up from everywhere inside her. She needed this man.

She wanted this man.

She took his hand and put it on the top of her head. Then she looked up at him, hoping to see in his eyes the same desire that filled her.

It was there. And for the first time since she arrived in Greece, she was happy. Completely happy.

He took her hand and pulled her to her feet, then he kissed her as she kissed him back.

To her the kiss seemed to last forever, and every instant was as wonderful as the one before it. At some point he led her into the hut and pushed her onto the bed.

Then for the next two hours he took her to places in her feelings, her body, her very soul, that she could have never imagined.

He was slow at times, gentle with her, stroking her skin, making her sigh with the gentleness of his touch.

Never had she been pushed so far, felt so satisfied, and so completely out of control.

She knew, now, without a doubt, that even if someone did come for them, she would never be the same.

And she knew that she never, ever wanted to leave Peppe.

He was her master. She was his slave.

He sat beside her, staring into the fire. She was wrapped in his arms, kissing him every few seconds, holding him as if she never wanted to let him go.

He had no intention of ever letting her go, either.

The lovemaking had been better than he might have thought it would be. She had taken everything he gave her and wanted more. She had delighted in his every touch, responded to his kisses, his hands. Her body gave all the promises of its looks.

She was a wild woman, a woman he knew he was a long way from even starting to tame, both in bed and in the real world.

He kissed her again, long and hard, then pulled back and looked into the love in her eyes. It was amazing to him how close the emotions of love and hate were. He had never started a relationship with hate before. But now he knew that love to hate was not the only way a relationship could go.

"You're so beautiful," he said, stroking her shoulder, looking at her skin in the yellow of the flickering fire. "You're a real woman."

She wiggled and squirmed in delight, moving in ways he didn't know a woman could move.

"I have never felt like this," she said.

"No," he said, smiling at her. "That's not right. You must call me 'master.' Yes, call me 'master.' I like that."

She smiled at him and kissed him hard, then eased back in his arms.

"My master," she said, her voice full and rich.

He rolled her over and lay on top of her, looking into her eyes.

At some point they ended up back in the hut, on the bed.

The next morning Amber could not believe how she felt. Never had she even imagined the lightness in her heart, the excitement of every chore, the desire to just be around one person. Peppe had become the center of her life in one day, and now everything took on new colors, new emotions.

The sunrise was something that she had never noticed before, filled with startling reds and oranges. The blueness of the ocean seemed deeper and more beautiful than she had remembered, as if a great artist had painted it. Around the camp the whiteness of the sand looked like diamonds glittering.

They did the fishing, she did the cleaning of the fish and cooking of breakfast while he lay on the sand in the early morning sun, napping.

She decided to try a slightly different way of cooking a fish, then took it to him with fresh water on a leaf.

He took a taste and frowned.

"Is it really bad?"

"Yes," he said, but she could tell he wasn't angry.

He took another bite, then looked up at her. "But you will get better."

"What have you done to me?" she asked gently, sitting down beside him and stroking his arm while he ate.

"What you needed doing to you," he said.

"I am no longer myself," she said, wanting to explain how she was feeling to the man she cared about more than anyone else. "I'm drunk. I feel like the Turks have taken me, pirates have abducted me, sheiks kidnapped me."

She kissed his arm, then looked into his eyes. "You are such a lover. It was incredible. How was it for you?"

She desperately wanted him to tell her it was as wonderful for him as it was for her.

"All right," he said, shrugging.

Then he laughed and she laughed with him.

"Back to being funny are we?" she asked. "Back to playing the com—"

He reached over and slapped her.

Her cheek stung and she was surprised. She put a hand on her cheek. The skin was hot where he had struck her.

"What's going on here?" he asked, looking at her. "What's with all the familiarity?"

"What happened to your humor?" she asked, smiling at him. "I was kidding."

"Kidding?" he asked. "Where did you get that idea? What were you thinking? You forgot your place."

She smiled at him and kissed his arm. Something about him being in complete control of her made her so excited, so hot for him, she didn't know what to do.

She didn't want to do anything, actually, except what he wanted her to do. Now that seemed to right, so perfect. She had no idea why she had fought him for so long.

"I am your master and I do the kidding," he said. "And I do the training. I'm the only one who understands you."

She nodded. "Yes, Master."

"Now come here and kiss me," he said, laughing as he pulled her up on top of him.

The kiss and lovemaking lasted long into the middle of the day.

And then later that night, and through the night, and into the next day.

She could not get enough of him and, for the first time in her life, wanted nothing more than what she had with him. Her life back in New York seemed like a distant dream, slowly being forgotten. And she didn't care.

Her world was now Peppe. And the island. And they were more than enough.

19

AMBER FELT AS IF THE LAST WEEK HAD BEEN THE BEST week of her life. In fact, she knew that her life had never really started until the last week.

As each day had gone by, Peppe had entrusted her with more and more duties, teaching her skills she never dreamed she could learn. Yesterday he had worked up a type of net fishing for her to do, and told her how to do it, and even showed her where to go to get the best-tasting fish.

One morning she had even caught an octopus and taken it to him in the shack. He had pretended to not care, but he was proud of her, she could tell.

Now, this morning as the sun peeked over the horizon, he had let her try her skill fishing on her own. She had gone to a spot on one of the rock outcroppings that jutted into the smooth blue water. There she had found a perfect place to cast the net, and then she had made what she thought was a great cast.

She was waiting, patiently, as he taught her, for the fish to gather over the net, when she happened to glance up at the sea. A boat was bearing down on the island, and looked as if it might land in the cove to her left.

She stood and was just about to wave excitedly at the boat, when another thought crossed her mind.

She didn't want to go.

She had never been so happy before. Why would she want to leave all this?

She wanted to stay right here, with Peppe, making love, enjoying the sun, catching fish and birds for food. She didn't need the streets of New York or her husband. She didn't need all the problems of being rich, of being bored, or having no love life.

She had everything she needed right here.

She slowly lowered herself back down and then eased over into a hole in the rocks where she could watch the boat but not be seen.

The boat was some sort of fast vessel that looked more like a Coast Guard ship off of New York than a yacht. She could see two men with binoculars scouring the shoreline. Clearly they were looking for something, and she had no doubt it was her and Peppe.

The boat turned just beyond the shallow reef,

going slowly along the shoreline of the island, its engines idling just loud enough to sound like distant thunder.

The boat worked its way to her left, the two men on board scanning the cove beside her, and then the cove beyond where they had landed.

She kept her head low and still. She just hoped that the dinghy was well enough hidden in the trees. Both sides had deflated after they moved it up off the beach. It would be hard to see, but still possible, she was sure. If they saw that they would come ashore and then she would have no choice. She would be rescued and have to go back, and right now that was not what she wanted. Not at all.

After a few minutes, the boat turned around and came back toward her, searching the shoreline along this side of the island where a raft would have landed, pushed by the winds and current.

She kept her head very low and still, almost afraid to breathe. If she screwed up now she would have to leave, and Peppe would be angry at her.

She wanted to stay with Peppe, right here in their own little world.

Finally she saw one of the men shake his head and indicate another direction.

The boat turned, and with a pretty loud roar headed off, spray splashing from its bow as it gained speed.

She waited in the rocks until she could no longer see the boat, then pulled up the net and three fishes besides.

Peppe could not get the thought out of his head of how her love for him would end if they left the island. With each passing day it had eaten at him, clawed at his stomach.

Amber on the other hand, did everything he said, was a perfect companion during the day, and passionate in love. She seemed to always be smiling, always putting flowers around their hut, always wanting to please him.

Now, as they sat together, working on the nets and looking out over the smooth ocean, his thoughts drifted back to the completeness of her love, and the doubts he had about it.

"What is wrong with you, Mr. Esposito?" she asked.

He looked down at the net in his hands. He'd been trying to fix it, but had not moved for the last few minutes because he'd been deep in thought. Across the beach a bird hopped along, pecking at the sand. The ocean today was smooth and bright blue, the day hot and dry.

"What are you wondering about?" he asked her. "You should learn to sew instead of talk."

He passed the fishing net on his lap to her.

"I love you," she said.

"Fine words," he said, letting his worry come to the surface. "But what if we hadn't been shipwrecked?"

She picked up the net and said nothing, studying the hole in it from a bad cast that had caught on rocks.

"You would still be a filthy rich, unhappy American," he said, pushing his fear into the light. "I would still be a happy, poor Italian without a place to live. You wouldn't have given me a thought. You would still be the grand lady, and I the smelly fisherman."

"That was before," she said, smiling at him. "Before I knew what it was like to love you."

He shook his head, even though he liked the sound of her words, wanted to hear her say those words. "It happened because we're here. The boundless passion is here, though I'd love to see Mrs. Amber strolling down Fifth Avenue with Mr. Esposito."

She smiled at him.

20

AMBER SAW THE SHIP FIRST AS IT ROUNDED THE END of the island. Peppe slept beside her. She watched it, hoping it would just go away as the other had done.

But then Peppe opened his eyes and saw it as well.

"Let's hide," she said, looking into Peppe's eyes, trying to see what he was thinking. "They won't see us if we are in our hut."

He stood and moved past her, toward the fire burning softly in front of their hut.

"Don't, Peppe," she said.

"Why not?" he asked, looking into her eyes. "You say you love me. I want the whole truth."

Amber could feel the tears starting to grow in her eyes. "What proof do you need?" she asked. "I have never been happier. We were meant to be together. You said so."

He nodded, clearly torn.

"I don't want to go back," she said. "I don't want to be tested. The two of us here, right now, are real."

She saw the tears come to Peppe's eyes as well. She wanted to go to him, hold him, take him to their hut so that they could hide until the boat passed.

"No," he said, shaking his head as she stepped toward him.

She stopped instantly, unable anymore to disobey him in any fashion.

"If you love me, you can love me anywhere," he said. "I want to know, have to know, if the wife of a rich man thinks the same as you."

She refused to let it go. "What do you care about where we are?"

He said nothing.

"Please, I beg of you to stay. I love you."

She stepped toward him and took his hand, holding it gently.

He took her hand out of his and shook his head. "I need proof. Then we can do as you say, but I need to know you can resist."

"Believe me," she said, the tears streaming down her face, "you are all I want."

He looked into her eyes, then asked, "You are scared, aren't you?"

She nodded.

The tears filled his eyes. "That's why I need the proof."

He turned and ran off.

She watched through her tears as he ran down toward the ship, waving his arms to attract attention.

She wanted to believe that she could still love Peppe when she got back to the real world. But inside there was a doubt. She might not be as smart as Peppe when it came to the ocean and fishing, but she knew the dangers of the real world.

And those dangers were much worse than anything found in this ocean. They were going to be lucky to survive, of that she had no doubt.

Their rescue ship was a large vacation cruiser that carried at least twenty guests and, Peppe guessed, a crew of ten. The ship was diesel powered and ran smoothly. There wasn't a surface that wasn't polished to a bright shine. Peppe had never worked aboard anything like it.

The captain, a thick Italian with a loud voice and hearty laugh, was standing among a number of his guests, waiting for lunch to start. All of the guests were firing questions at Amber. Peppe stood off to one side, ignored.

"My God," one lady said, "what did you do for food?"

"We made do," Amber said, smiling. "Mr. Esposito was very clever."

"But for so long?" another man asked, clearly amazed.

Peppe watched as the captain glanced around and saw him, then waved him over. "Come on and eat with me," he said.

With one glance at Amber standing in the middle of the crowd of rich people, he followed the captain into a private cabin.

The man handed Peppe a large cigar and then thanked the steward who brought him and Peppe fine soup and sandwiches. After a diet of only fish and birds, the cigar and soup and sandwich tasted wonderful.

"How did things go with the lady?" the captain asked, smiling and winking at Peppe.

Peppe knew what he meant. "She's a good girl," he said. "Nothing happened."

"Really?" the captain asked, shocked. "Nothing? You are a stronger man than me. Over a month on a deserted island, and she is not bad looking."

The captain shook his head and took another bite of his sandwich.

"You know," he said while chewing, "the whole world has been looking for you."

Peppe shrugged. He had assumed as much, considering how much money she had.

"Her husband's going to reward you," the captain said. "We called him on the radio. He's going to meet us at the dock at our next stop later today. He hasn't left the islands."

Peppe's stomach twisted. This had been a mistake, he knew it now. He had been as stupid as she was. Yet he couldn't let the doubt eat at him. He had to know, but the problem was, knowing more than likely meant losing her.

Three hours later the cruise liner worked its way toward the sturdy dock of a large harbor. Houses were scattered up the rock hills above the harbor, and Peppe knew there was a large downtown area and a number of hotels. This place was a popular tourist stop both for large tour boats and others flying in.

Tony's helicopter was there, sitting next to one of the hotels on the harbor like a big bird. Tony was standing on the dock, looking calm and collected. He wore a jacket and slacks, but no tie. Standing there, he seemed much more powerful than Peppe had remembered him to be.

It took what seemed like an eternity for the boat to get docked and the gangway lowered. Then Tony moved up and hugged Amber as Peppe watched.

Peppe could see the look on her face. It wasn't happiness, but it wasn't despair, either. She didn't push Tony away. It was exactly what he had feared would happen. She didn't love Peppe enough to cut all ties and come with him.

"Mr. Esposito," Amber's husband said, breaking away from his hug on her. He extended his hand to Peppe. "I want to thank you for saving my wife. She said you were very decent."

Peppe stared at the man for a moment. The man who was standing there with his arms around the woman Peppe loved. What could be said at a moment like that?

Peppe nodded and turned away, walking for the stairs that led up into the city.

A man wearing a suit jumped out of a car and met Peppe halfway across the small parking lot.

"Mr. Esposito," the man said, falling in beside Peppe as he walked, "we are very grateful for your assistance and help. We have even provided a room in the hotel for you to rest and recuperate."

Peppe just ignored him. There was nothing he could say.

After a moment the man stopped and turned away, letting Peppe go.

How could this have happened? Why had he been so stupid, not believing her when she said she wanted to stay on the island? Why had he forced her back into her husband's arms? There was no doubt that she knew more than he knew.

He walked the short distance to the hotel bar, then went inside and stood at the bar. He didn't know what to do, what to even drink. His mind was spinning. He had to get her away from her husband and back to the island.

If she wanted to go. He had to believe she did.

He had to.

"Mr. Esposito," someone said behind him.

Peppe turned to see the same man who worked for Amber's husband.

"There is one other thing," the man said. "Can we sit down?"

Peppe said nothing and remained standing by the bar.

"As a reflection of our appreciation," the man said after a moment, "we would like to give you this."

Peppe took the man and the case he was trying to offer him and ran him back out the door and into the street. The case dropped onto the cobblestones and the man stumbled a moment before catching his balance and turning to face Peppe.

"I do not want your bribes," Peppe said, kicking the case at the man.

"It's not a bribe, Mr. Esposito," the man said.

He turned and walked away, leaving the case on the street in front of Peppe.

After a moment Peppe moved over and bent down and looked into the case. It was completely full of money. A lot of money. More than he had ever seen in one place at one time.

He stared at it for a moment, then slowly a plan

started to form. A plan to get Amber back with him, and the two of them away from her husband and all his money.

Within one hour Peppe had used her husband's money to buy the most expensive ring he could find in town.

And then he started calling her.

And calling.

And calling.

She never returned his calls, and as the days went by, he got more and more panicked. And more afraid.

Amber had never been so miserable. How could Peppe do this to her? She had been so happy on the island, so peaceful, so content with life. Yet he had forced her to leave, to come back to Tony, to this world.

And now she didn't know what to do. Peppe wasn't around to tell her.

The greeting with Tony had been uncomfortable at best. He had asked a few questions about the month, had been clearly happy to see her, and then within a few hours the two of them had lapsed back into old patterns. They only talked in one word sentences and she bossed him around.

She hated that, hated herself, hated Tony for allowing it. Why had Peppe forced her to do this?

When Tony realized that she was healthy, after the doctor he had flown in had given her a full check-up, he had insisted that they go out to a nice dinner to celebrate her return.

She had tried to say no, but he had made her feel guilty, telling her about all the time he had spent looking for her, how much he had sacrificed at work, how much money he had spent in the search, how much he had paid Peppe for his services.

The last statement had sent a cold chill through her heart.

Tony kept at her. The least she could do was go have a nice dinner with him.

At dinner they had run out of things to talk about almost instantly. She didn't want to tell him what had happened on the island and he didn't ask. They were headed back through the lobby when the desk clerk said, "Phone call for you, madam."

Tony looked surprised.

Amber felt the same way. "Me?"

"Yes, madam," the clerk said, indicating that she should take the call to one side of the lobby.

"I'll go on and wait for you," Tony said.

The area was fairly dark, and had windows that overlooked the harbor. She picked up the phone and said, "Yes?"

"It's me."

Amber wanted to shout, to scream for joy. His

voice was the best she had ever heard. It made her heart sing, her breath shorten.

"Why did you wait so long to call?"

"I have called," he said.

She glanced around the lobby, looking at the clerk behind the desk. "They didn't tell me."

"It doesn't matter," Peppe said, his voice full of emotion. "I love you."

She waited a second.

"I love you," he said, again. "I love you more than I ever thought possible. You are in charge now. I am yours. I always will be."

The words she had said to him on the island sounded so right, so impossibly right coming to her now.

"I love you, too, my darling," she said. "More than life."

The tears were starting to flow, even though she didn't dare let them flow here, at this point, at this time.

Then, as she feared would happen, Tony walked back into the lobby and glanced at her. She tried to turn her head away so that he wouldn't see her eyes, but the short phone cord would not let her turn too far.

"My husband is coming," she whispered. "Leave a message at reception, tell me what to do, and I'll do it."

She hung up the phone, wiped her eyes as unobtrusively as she could, and then turned.

Tony was gone. But it didn't matter. Peppe loved her, they were going to be together, and that was all that mattered.

Peppe sat for the hour after the phone call in the corner of a local bar, writing her a carefully worded note, making sure he was very clear on what she needed to do. She was to come to a certain boat on the pier. It was a friend's boat, someone who could be trusted to never speak of word of where he took them. It had already been set up that they were going back to the island.

Back to the place where they had both been happy.

After he finished the note, he put the ring he had bought her into the small envelope, sealed it, and walked the five blocks to the hotel.

A woman stood behind the reception desk.

"May I leave a message for a guest?"

"Of course," she said.

He took the envelope out and handed it to her. "This can only go to Mrs. Leighton. Not her husband, or anyone else. Understand?"

She looked at him like he was crazy, then nodded.

She moved over and put the note into a slot high on the board behind her, leaving one end sticking out so anyone could see.

"No," Peppe said. "Move it back farther and only give it to her."

The woman nodded and pushed the brown envelope back even farther, so that it was mostly out of sight.

Peppe stared at it for a moment, wishing his entire future happiness was in a little more secure place, then turned and headed for the docks. He had things to get ready, provisions to put on the boat.

They would cast off not longer than ten seconds after she stepped on the boat, and he had to be ready. It was going to be a long night.

Amber awoke to find her husband gone from the bed. Her heart seemed to skip a beat as she jumped up and grabbed her robe and headed for the reception desk downstairs.

She had to find out what Peppe had told her to do, had to know what the future would bring.

She made it out of the room without seeing her husband and to the front desk.

"Any messages for me?" she asked the man standing there.

He looked at her robe and then started to turn to check the messages.

"Amber," her husband said behind her, "What are you doing down here?"

She turned to face the surprise on his face as he saw her in her robe.

"I was looking for you," she said, covering quickly.

"Oh," he said. "Well, you need to get dressed. We're leaving soon."

She nodded as he turned to the desk clerk. "Any messages for us?"

The clerk pulled a piece of paper out of the slot and handed it to her husband. It was clearly a message, but she couldn't tell from who.

Her husband read it, then nodded. "It's from the office. He glanced at the desk clerk. "I need to make a call."

The desk clerk picked up a phone and set it on the counter.

She stared at the message in his hand, then nodded and went to get dressed. She was sure that if he had gotten the message from Peppe, he would have let on.

Which meant that Peppe had not yet sent her a message. Or was never going to.

She moved slowly out of the reception area, all the energy and excitement that had been there a few moments before gone.

What was Peppe doing? Why hadn't he left her a note?

Tony stood at the front desk and watched his wife in her robe leave the room. There was no doubt in his mind that she and the Italian sailor had had an affair of some sort. But he was going to make sure that it stayed on that island.

And the first thing to make sure of that was to get her home, back to New York, where she belonged.

He stared to punch in the number he needed on the phone when he saw in their mail slot something the clerk had not picked out, something tucked back farther.

He pointed up at the package. "There's something in my mail," he said to the clerk.

"Oh, I'm sorry, sir," the clerk said, getting the small envelope and handing it to Tony.

Tony put the phone down and opened the envelope. An expensive diamond ring dropped out into his hand, and a note from Peppe, telling Amber where to go to meet him.

It was signed, "I love you always."

Those words echoed in his mind. This could not be allowed. No one was going to take Amber from him. No one.

And especially someone like Peppe.

He put the ring back in the envelope with the note and then wrote the number of the boat slip on the outside of the envelope and stuck both in his pocket.

Three hours later, he managed to get his wife to the waiting helicopter. She seemed to be walking in slow motion, looking around everywhere, clearly for her sailor.

Tony had made sure that wasn't going to happen. He had moved up their scheduled departure by hours, and there didn't seem to be anything Amber was trying to do to stop it besides waiting.

And since the note from her lover was in his pocket, Tony knew that she would be waiting a long time.

After they had climbed into the chopper and the bellboy had stored the last bags, Tony took out a hundred-dollar bill and put it under the envelope, with the slip number down.

Then he handed the envelope to Amber, who seemed to be almost sleepwalking.

"Honey," he said over the sound of the chopper engines warming up. "Would you give this tip to the bellboy?"

She took the envelope and then seemed to stop, as if not really hearing him.

"The boy," he said, nudging her. "Would you give him the tip?"

She nodded and handed the boy the envelope and the money.

The boy nodded and closed the door.

Tony watched as the boy stepped away from the helicopter, turned the envelope over, stuffed the money in his pocket, and then started to walk toward the piers.

Tony had no doubt that would end all thoughts of Peppe coming after her, especially when the boy said she had given him the envelope.

Tony sat back beside his wife. She might be unhappy, she might be a bitch at times, but she was still his wife, and she belonged at his side in New York. And now nothing was going to change that.

21

PEPPE'S FRIEND WAITED ON HIS BOAT, THE MOTOR running, as Peppe paced on the dock. The afternoon air was warm, the sky clear. A perfect day for a romantic escape to a deserted island.

He could imagine the two of them going back to the island and living for years and years. He had even set up arrangements for a regular food drop of flour and other basics with his friend. He had purchased medical supplies with the last of Amber's husband's money, and an emergency radio, too. All that was now safely packed onto the boat, ready to take them back to their home.

He paced, letting the air calm him as the fear ate at him. This was the very thing he had worried about. Now he knew his worry, and hers, had been accurate. He should have been smart enough to just leave it all alone, hide from the boats, and stay in control of her. But he had not done that. He had been stupid.

From out of the shadows, a young bellboy appeared, strolling up to Peppe.

"No, no, no," Peppe said as the boy extended his hand.

In the boy's grasp was the envelope with the ring Peppe had left for Amber. Peppe's future, his dreams, and all his love were in that envelope.

He asked the boy where he had gotten it. He told him a woman in a helicopter had given it to him.

She had sent it all back to him.

How could she have done that?

He had to know.

He had to confront her, even if her husband tossed him in jail for bothering her.

Peppe had to know why. She owed him that much.

He took the envelope and ring from the boy and started running toward the hotel. It was only a few blocks, but it felt as if it were forever. All the way, thoughts about how stupid he had been to let her go filled his mind. She had begged him to not do it, but, thinking he was so smart, he had forced her back into the arms of her husband.

Into the world of money.

What could a poor man with only a deserted island offer to match that?

Now he knew the answer was nothing.

Suddenly the sound of a helicopter powering up as its engines filled the air.

"No!" he shouted, running even faster.

He swerved to the back of the hotel, jumped over a hedge, and sprinted around a pool. The helicopter was sitting near the seawall, its black and white shape a sign of doom to him.

He couldn't believe what he saw as he rounded the last corner of the bathhouse. Both Tony and Amber were in the helicopter.

As the blades picked up speed he ran up but he was too late. It lifted from the ground and slowly turned.

Inside he could see Amber crying, doing her best to conceal it from her husband.

Tony was sitting, facing forward, ignoring Peppe and his wife as if they didn't exist for him.

The pilot saw Peppe and glanced at Tony.

"Amber!" Peppe shouted, but the sound from the helicopter drowned his voice as if it the word had never been spoken.

Tony nodded to the pilot, and the helicopter took off, pulling away slowly out over the water.

Inside Peppe could see Amber, staring ahead, into a future without him.

At that moment he knew all his fears back on the island had been correct.

She would have eventually grown tired of him and the island.

He thought she had loved him, but perhaps she only knew how to control or be controlled. She controlled Tony, Peppe controlled her. Peppe, by not hiding from that boat, had given her the choice of being the slave or the master, and she had chosen to be the master.

It made sense.

It was the same choice he had made over her. He had been the slave, but when given the chance, he had become the master.

Now he was back where he belonged.

And she was back where she belonged.

He took the ring out of his pocket as the helicopter turned away; he threw the ring at her.

It bounced off the window right in front of her face. A moment later the ring splashed in the harbor and vanished.

A moment later he was again alone.